SERIES PRAISE FOR BARRY FORBES

AMAZING BOOK! My daughter is in 6th grade and she is homeschooled, she really enjoyed reading this book. Highly recommend to middle schoolers. *Rubi Pizarro on Amazon*

I have three boys 11-15 and finding a book they all like is sometimes a challenge. This series is great! My 15-year-old said, "I actually like it better than Hardy Boys because it tells me currents laws about technology that I didn't know." My reluctant 13-year-old picked it up without any prodding and that's not an easy feat. *Shantelshomeschool on Instagram*

I stumbled across the author and his series on Instagram and had to order the first book! Fun characters, good storyline too, easy reading. Best for ages 11 and up. *AZmommy2011 on Amazon*

Virtues of kindness, leadership, compassion, responsibility, loyalty, courage, diligence, perseverance, loyalty and service are characterized throughout the book. *Lynn G. on Amazon*

Barry, he LOVED it! My son is almost 14 and enjoys reading but most books are historical fiction or non-fiction. He carried your book everywhere, reading in any spare moments. He can't wait for book 2 – I'm ordering today and book 3 for his birthday. *Ourlifeathome on Instagram*

Perfect series for our 7th grader! I'm thrilled to have come across this perfect series for my 13-year old son this summer. We purchased the entire set! They are easy, but captivating reads and he is enjoying them very much. *Amylcarney on Amazon*

THE SECRETS OF THE MYSTERIOUS MANSION

A MYSTERY SEARCHERS BOOK

BARRY FORBES

THE SECRETS OF THE MYSTERIOUS MANSION

A MYSTERY SEARCHERS BOOK

VOLUME 3

By
BARRY FORBES

ST. LEO PRESS

The Secrets of the Mysterious Mansion © 2019 Barry Forbes

Copyright notice: All rights reserved under the International and Pan-American Copyright Conventions. No part of this book may be reproduced or transmitted in any form or by any means, electronic or mechanical, including photocopying, recording, or by any information storage and retrieval system, without permission in writing from the publisher.

Warning: the unauthorized reproduction or distribution of this copyrighted work is illegal. Criminal copyright infringement, including infringement without monetary gain, is investigated by the FBI and is punishable by up to 5 years in prison and a fine of $250,000.

DISCLAIMER

Prescott, the former capital of the Arizona Territory, is considered by many to be the state's crown jewel. Aside from this central Arizona locale, *The Mystery Searchers* series is a work of fiction. Names, characters, businesses, places, events, incidents, and other locales are either the products of the author's imagination or used in a fictitious manner. Any resemblance to actual persons, living or dead, or actual events is purely coincidental.

Read more at www.MysterySearchers.com

For Linda,
whose steadfast love and encouragement
made this series possible

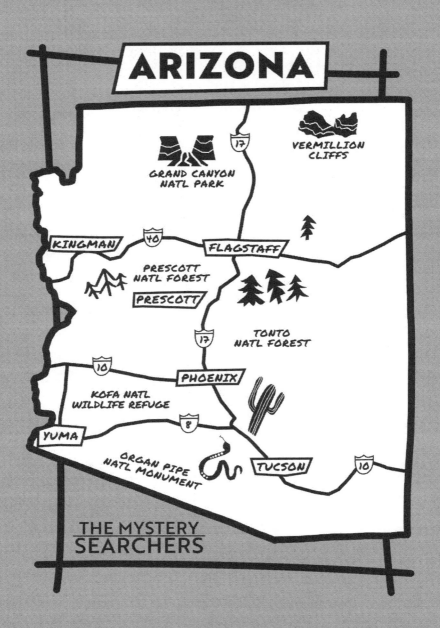

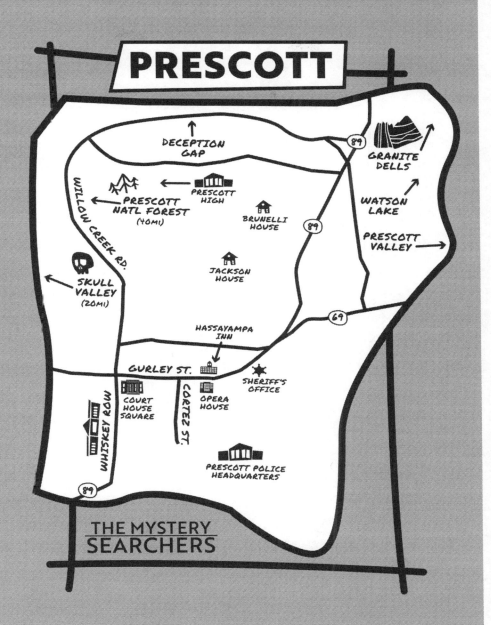

1

THE FINDING

It was a frigid winter night in the high country of Prescott, Arizona. A dusting of snow, whipped by howling winds, swirled around the Chevy. The reading on the dashboard thermometer continued to drop. Poor driving conditions became worse as the car —buffeted all the way down Route 69—made slow progress. Its windshield wipers beat a rhythmic tune in a vain struggle at visibility.

Heidi Hoover sat in the backseat, peering into the churning darkness, searching for a hidden turnoff. *"There!"* she cried out, pointing through the window on the driver's side. "We almost missed it. There it is."

Tom Jackson—quiet, thoughtful, and steady as a rock—gripped the steering wheel with both hands and cranked a sudden left. The Chevy bumped and bounced over frozen ruts onto a rough dirt road.

"You're sure?" Tom's twin sister, Suzanne, asked. She tightened her front passenger seat belt, staring hard at the bleak scene before her.

Heidi laughed. "Don't worry, Suzie. I drove out here before. Half a mile of this, and then we'll go for a *nice* walk." The way she said it didn't sound nice at all.

Heidi had attended Prescott High, graduating a few years ahead of the twins and their best friends, Kathy and Pete Brunelli. During the time they had all overlapped at school, the four had barely known Heidi. She was a young child—her family refugees from civil war in Mozambique—when they settled in Prescott.

After college, she had landed a job with Prescott's hometown newspaper, *The Daily Pilot*. A short, cute-featured young woman with tight black curls and a dynamic personality, she had soon emerged as the newspaper's star reporter.

Earlier that Thursday evening, Heidi had called Suzanne on her cell phone. "I've got something that's perfect for you guys," she said. "Let's go for a ride—tonight. But make sure you dress for warmth. It's freezing cold out there."

"*Tonight?*" Suzanne had replied. "It's awfully late. Out where?"

Heidi knew Suzie as a confident, assured person who knew where she was going in life—someone willing to tackle new challenges. Even better, the Jackson twins were half of the four-person mystery searchers team. "*There*. Trust me, the trip will be worthwhile."

The twins would miss having their best friends tag along, but the Brunelli siblings were out of town. The Jacksons and Brunellis had grown up together, and over the years, their families had become exceptionally close. Today, the four were all out from Prescott High for the Christmas break. The Brunellis wouldn't return from an extended gathering of their cousins until the next day—Friday, December twenty-seventh.

"They'll miss out," Tom had said to his sister, lacing up his warm winter boots. The family Christmas tree—harvested from a Prescott forest and still brightly lit—towered above them in the living room.

"Can't help it," Suzanne had said. "Let's go."

The twins picked Heidi up at her apartment on the city's west side. She jumped into the backseat and pointed the way to Route 69.

"Okay, you're being a little mysterious," Suzanne said, turning around in her seat to face Heidi. "Give us a clue."

"We're about to visit a deserted mansion in the forest," Heidi teased. "From a distance."

Suzanne's eyes grew larger. "A *deserted* mansion?"

"From a distance?" Tom asked. "Why not tour the place?"

"You'll soon find out."

The Jackson twins, together with Pete and Kathy, had earned a local reputation for mystery solving. Heidi had covered their two previous cases for the newspaper: the mystery on Apache Canyon Drive, and the ghost in the county courthouse. Both had been front-page news—and not just in Prescott.

Along the way, Heidi had become one of the foursome's biggest fans. "You stick to a case like chewing gum," she had once told them. "You never give up. I like that. As a reporter that's just what I do too."

Heidi was also a fan of the twins' father, Edward Jackson—*Chief* Edward Jackson of the Prescott City Police. Most people considered him the most popular chief in the city's history. Heidi agreed. "Fair and honest," she replied whenever anyone asked. "Plus, he knows what he's doing. What's not to like?"

The road was soon close to impassable. Heidi tapped Tom on the shoulder. "Okay, park it. This is the end."

"Here?" Tom asked, slowing to a stop. There was no room to pull over. "In the middle of the road?"

"Uh-huh," Heidi replied. "It's a track, not a road. Believe me, no one's coming behind you. From here, we walk."

Three car doors swung open. The wind whistled through the Chevy, blitzing its occupants with driving snow.

"Whoa, this is *seriously* cold!" Suzanne exclaimed, shivering as she tightened a scarf and zipped up her parka. The twins had both brought thick gloves too; they needed them.

"Told you," Heidi said, chuckling out loud. She buttoned up her big jacket and grabbed her camera bag, leading the way into the night. "You'll warm up soon enough. Follow me."

"How far is the mansion?" Tom shouted into the wind.

"Just two blocks as the crow flies!" Heidi yelled back. "But this crazy path twists and turns on the way there."

Silence descended as the three hikers trekked onward. The rough trail, slippery with fresh-frozen ice under the blowing snow, sloped uphill—so narrow that it allowed passage for only one person at a time. It was slow going.

Tom, breathing hard, drew near to Heidi. "Is this the only way in?"

"Nope, there's a quicker route—an old mining road, but we need to avoid it." She didn't say why, but the county was famous for its gold, silver, copper, lead, and zinc mines—most long abandoned.

Suzanne gazed up into a spectacular night sky to see a million stars twinkling back at her. The biting wind had died away—towering trees provided a degree of shelter—but at ground level it was cold, dark, and dreary. Still, the exertion generated welcome body heat.

Heidi came to a sudden halt and pointed. "Okay, we're going up this hill."

A minute later, they stopped. Long moments passed while the three of them caught their breath. They stood on a hilltop, well above the tree line, gazing at a bleak vista across which eddies of swirling snow ebbed and flowed. Scudding clouds, illuminated fitfully by a waxing moon, raced overhead. Below, a dark forest of stately ponderosa pine circled them, stretching out as far as they could see.

Temperatures continued to drop as the wind kicked up again, hammering the bare, shelter-less hill, gusting in bursts and winding its way down through the sentinel-like trees.

Heidi knelt and opened her camera case. "We're here."

Suzanne locked eyes with her brother. "We don't get it, Heidi. When you say, 'here'..."

Heidi set up a tripod in seconds and attached her camera to it. She stood up. "Look right where I'm pointing. What do you see?"

"Trees!" the twins chorused.

Heidi giggled. "No. Check out the *next* ridge. Notice how the line of trees has a horizontal flat edge running through its center?"

"Oh, wow, yes—I see it now," Suzanne said. "Just faintly."

"Me too," Tom said. "Straight as an arrow."

"Yes, it is. That's the mansion's roofline," Heidi replied. She knelt again to lock the tripod down and focus the camera. She had loaded it with infrared film to capture images in the dark. "Okay, that works. Now relax. Based on my experience over the last two nights, we won't have long to wait."

"Wait for what?" Suzanne asked.

"You'll see."

"You were here the last two nights?" Tom asked incredulously.

"At midnight? *By yourself?*" Suzanne couldn't believe it.

"Yes, and I'll tell you why." The twins crouched down, close on the ground beside Heidi. Suzanne wrapped her arms around her knees for warmth. Long strands of auburn hair blew across her face. She pulled her hood tighter.

"My neighbor is a gold bug—he's panned out here for years. Never laid eyes on the place. Know why? Over time, trees and bushes had surrounded this mansion in the forest—like Sleeping Beauty's castle. It was like, well, *buried*. Last week he stumbled onto it by accident. He walked into a clearing, and there it was." She paused, surveying the scene before them. "He couldn't believe it. Later that night he called me. Next morning, I drove out here. *I couldn't believe it*. You can stand fifty yards away and never see the place."

Heidi stopped again, blowing on her hands for warmth before thrusting them into her pockets. "I scouted around. Bushes had grown across the back door, but someone had cut a narrow channel through them. Not long before, either—the chop marks on the branches were fresh. I knew I wasn't the first person out here."

"Was it locked?" Tom asked.

"Nope. Nor the front door or the garage. They didn't lock a thing."

"Who's 'they'?" Tom asked.

"Keep your eyes on the mansion while we talk," Heidi said. She had an annoying habit of ignoring questions. "You don't want to miss this."

Suzanne asked, "Miss what?"

"After getting in, I toured the place," Heidi continued. "I was careful not to disturb anything—I crept around, quiet like a mouse. But the shots I got with my camera are unbelievable. Someone walked out of there decades ago... *and never returned.* I found a newspaper spread out on the kitchen table. It was from nineteen eighty-nine."

"You mean they left the table behind—their furniture?" Tom asked.

Heidi looked at him for a long moment. He wasn't getting it. "They sure did. And everything else too. And I mean *everything*." She paused again. "Furniture, silverware, dishes, bedding. Pictures on the walls, family photographs, personal documents, you name it. And that was just the main floor," Heidi continued. "Same story up and down. The place is huge. Creeped me right out."

The twins' minds reeled: a deserted, *abandoned* mansion in the forest. *Why?*

"Weren't you frightened?" Suzanne asked. She couldn't imagine herself walking through a dark, deserted place alone, day or night. Though with Kathy or Pete or her brother—different story...

"Freaked, not frightened," Heidi replied. "But I'll tell you something strange. I *knew* that I wasn't alone. At first, I figured it was my imagination, but I couldn't shake the feeling. It was like a sixth sense."

Suzanne blanched. "Well, that's creepy enough."

"What happened to the people who lived there?" Tom asked.

"That's why you're here," Heidi said, a half smile crossing her face in the dark. "I don't have the answers, but you guys are mystery searchers, and you're good at it. This is big, and it's right up your alley. In fact, my editor thinks this is page-one material. But he wants background. Who were these people? What happened to them? Why did they walk away from everything? And where did they go?"

The trio sat in silence for a couple more minutes, their minds racing.

"Maybe they didn't need this place anymore—" Tom began.

Just then, Heidi stiffened and cried out in a raw whisper. *"There it is!"*

2

A LATE-NIGHT INTRUDER

The three rocketed to their feet, staring into the darkness. A light had appeared along the tree line, almost at the level of the mansion's roof, rotating in an arc from left to right.

The hair rose on the back of their necks. Even Heidi—witnessing the event for a third time—said she felt spooked. The light flickered on and off and bobbed up and down.

Suzanne spoke first, her voice cracking. "Okay, now I'm scared."

"Wh—what is that?" Tom stammered.

"From here it looks as if it's in the trees," Heidi whispered. "But it's not. We're looking at the top floor of the mansion. He's inside."

Suzanne's eyes remained locked on the scene before them, but she grabbed her brother's arm. "*He?* Who is he?" she hissed.

"And what's he doing in there?" Tom wondered, his voice dropping lower.

"Why are we whispering?" Heidi asked, giggling once more. "No way can he hear us." The trio emitted a nervous laugh.

"Are you sure it's a '*he*'?" Tom asked.

"Yup," Heidi replied.

"And you're sure you *weren't* alone in that house?" Suzanne asked.

"Go figure, right?" Heidi said. "I scared him off—whoever he was. Just as I walked into the garage, the back door closed—no mistaking that sound. I mean, how crazy is that? So right away, I *knew* I wasn't alone."

Shivers traveled up and down Suzanne's spine.

Heidi stopped, seeming to replay the scene in her mind. "He took off. The old mining road is the only way in or out. Pretty much a road to nowhere. So I figured he'd be back. I returned that same night, but first I scouted around. After I found the track we took, I hiked up here."

"You didn't want to run into him," Suzanne said.

"You got that right."

The wind gusted even stronger. Heidi grabbed the tripod, making sure it wouldn't budge, and set the camera to auto. It clicked softly every thirty seconds. Somehow, the repetitive sound grounded the trio, reassuring them. *Nothing to worry about. It'll be okay.*

"So I camped here, on this hill, at eleven p.m. The light appeared just after midnight. Creeped me right out." Heidi blew on her hands. "I mean, think about it. Who's touring a deserted mansion in the middle of the night? He spent an hour searching around in there."

"Everywhere?" Tom asked.

"You bet. Ground floor, upstairs, you name it. I swear he searched every room." She paused a few moments. "I took a lot of pics when I was inside. The place is like a museum. Time stopped in nineteen eighty-nine. Wait 'til you see what's in the garage. Blew me away."

As Heidi talked, beams of light scattered through the windows. "I came back the second night. Same time too. An hour later *two* guys showed up. One searched upstairs while the other guy explored the main floor. Every so often it looked like they'd meet up, just for a minute or two—the light beams would appear in adjacent windows. I figured they were comparing notes. Then a light clicked off. I thought they were shutting down for the night. Next thing I know, someone is out front—in silhouette. A shadow. He aimed his flashlight toward the roofline, right where the gutters are, and circled the mansion."

"Did you move closer to get a look at them?" Tom asked.

"Are you *serious*?" Heidi said, glaring at him in the darkness. "I might be brave, but I'm not stupid. My guess is that anyone roaming around a deserted mansion at midnight is armed. In fact, I'd be willing to bet on it."

Suzanne asked again. "But who are they? What are they looking for?"

"No clue," Heidi replied. "But whatever it is, they haven't found it, have they?"

Twenty minutes later, the flashlight clicked off for good. Utter darkness returned to the mansion.

"Don't move yet," Heidi counseled. "Wait until his car starts up. We need to make sure."

Not long after, the sound of an ignition carried though the forest.

"He's done," Heidi said, packing up her camera equipment. "And I'll bet he's leaving empty-handed. Let's get out of here."

"Whoever this guy is, he took the other road in, right?" Suzanne asked.

"He sure did," Heidi replied, raising her voice as she headed down the hill. "He reached the end of the road and parked his car in the forest. Then he walked the last few hundred yards. It's easy if you know how. Plus, there's a million places to park in the trees where no one can spot you. I doubt if he's even aware of the trail we're on."

The three hikers lapsed into silence. So many questions, and not a single answer. Who had lived there so long ago? Why did they disappear? Where did they go? *And why did they leave everything behind?*

The twins' minds spun. There wasn't anything they relished more than a mystery. As the children of the local chief of police, they had always enjoyed a front-row seat at the family dining room table.

"Who did it, Dad?" they'd ask. "Were there clues? Can you catch them?"

Often, the Chief couldn't say a word. During an investigation, the department's work was confidential. No exceptions. With almost all the facts concealed, an obscuring fog kept everyone in the family guessing. Someday, the twins were certain, they would both follow their father into law enforcement.

The trek back to their vehicle was all downhill. The only sounds were their footsteps falling along the frozen path and rasping breath. At some point it dawned on Suzanne that she was no longer cold. The temperature had continued to drop, but under her parka she was sweating.

Weird mysteries do that to you, she thought. And this one was seriously weird.

3

THE TIME CAPSULE

Kathy cheered. "Another adventure begins!"

The Brunellis—with their coal-dark hair, olive-hued skin and Italian to the core—had arrived home the previous evening. Shorter and a little heavier than their tall, willowy friends, they looked enough alike to be mistaken for twins. The foursome had been inseparable since their early days at elementary school.

It hadn't taken long for the four mystery searchers to hatch a plan.

"*Someone* is after *something*—and they're undertaking an extensive search," Pete said, rubbing his hands together in glee. He couldn't wait.

"Day after day," Tom said.

"Night after night," Suzanne corrected. "And after midnight, which is freaky weird."

Whatever *something* was, they wanted to find it first. Scouting the mansion was imperative—and the sooner, the better. By ten o'clock Saturday morning, they headed north on Route 69.

"I'm telling you, this one is eerie," Suzanne said, turning toward her friends in the backseat. Imagined night scenes of the mysterious mansion filtered through her mind. Then something caught her eye. "Kathy, is that a *new* cell phone?"

"Sure is. My Christmas gift from mom and dad. Here, check it out."

"How far is it out there?" Pete asked.

Tom replied, "Twenty minutes at most."

The sun peeked out through the clouds. A thin layer of new morning snow had long since melted away. The wind had died off, only to return in bursts, chilling the unwary.

The twins occupied the front seat with Tom at the wheel. Pete and Kathy sat in the back, hunched forward toward their best friends, excited with anticipation.

"There are two roads in," Tom said, glancing in the rearview mirror. "We're taking the easier one."

"What makes it easier?" Pete asked.

Suzanne turned around and stifled a laugh, recalling Friday night. "Well, the other one isn't an actual road. It's more like a track."

"That's a fact," Tom agreed. He explained why Heidi had chosen the rough route. "She didn't want to alert the hunters. But during the daytime, she thinks the other road should be fine."

"She scared them off... and doesn't expect them back in daylight," Suzanne said. "We're hoping she's right."

"Me too," Kathy said. "'The 'hunters'? That's what she calls them?"

"You bet," Tom replied. "And until we know what they're hunting, we'll do our level best to avoid them too."

"There's no address for this place," Suzanne said, tracking their progress on Google Maps with her cell phone, "but Heidi sent us the coordinates."

Tom turned off Route 69 onto a little-traveled dirt road, right where Heidi had pegged it. The road dead-ended at the half-mile mark, where he pulled into the forest and stopped. A sea of green swallowed their vehicle, making it invisible from the road.

"Okay," Tom said, opening his door. "Let's go. We're close."

The four of them followed a winding, overgrown path for a few hundred yards. They hiked through a deep stand of rugged ponderosa pine before stepping into an open clearing. Heidi was right. A person could linger fifty yards from the mansion and never see it. But step into the open and there it was—a magnificent sight.

Over time, the forest had cloaked the palatial structure, but up close it rose, majestic and once proud.

"An unbelievable beauty," Kathy said, subdued and astonished in equal measure. Strands of English ivy shrouded the gray stone exterior walls, stretching high to the roofline. "It reminds me of a fortification from long ago, strong and safe from invaders."

"That would be us," Pete said.

"Yes, it's more like a castle than a mansion," Suzanne said. She guessed the two-story structure had to contain five or six thousand square feet of space.

"I can't imagine anyone deserting this place," Tom said, admiring its immense rectangular shape and architectural design.

Overgrown vines stretched from ground to roofline, encasing gigantic front-facing windows in greenery. Fifteen-foot-high hedges on either side of the grand double doors blocked the entranceway, rendering them impassible.

They circled to the rear of the home, passing three giant side-by-side garage doors with peeling faded-green paint. A thicket of bushes, cut away at its center, obstructed the back entrance.

Tom ducked in and turned the handle. The door swung open. "Okay, we're in."

They stepped onto a spacious landing. A musty odor assaulted their senses, and a damp chill hung in the stillness. To their left, the landing connected to a large kitchen. A right turn led to a central hallway.

In complete silence, open-mouthed, the foursome turned left.

Natural light filtered through yellow kitchen curtains. Tom flipped a wall switch. Nothing. A newspaper—a copy of the *Arizona Republic*—lay across a small breakfast table. The headline on the front page read, "Alaska hit by sharp quake." Beside the paper rested a stained coffee cup, dusty and dry. Someone had pushed a wooden kitchen chair away at a right angle.

Suzanne checked the newspaper's date: Tuesday, March 21, 1989. She spoke out loud without realizing it. "Drank coffee and read the newspaper… and then left, never to return. Wow."

They felt like intruders, strangers treading into someone else's private life, which—in an odd way—they were.

The kitchen cupboards were ajar, packed with dishes stacked in neat, even rows. Arrayed in open drawers were silverware, utensils, napkins, and place mats. Underneath were more cupboards, doors asunder, pots and pans forced aside.

Dishes lay on the counter next to the sink—two plates, a cereal bowl, one cup, some silverware. The dishware, set upside down and ready for drying, surely hadn't been moved in decades.

"Spooky," Kathy said, not daring to touch a thing.

A Hall's Hardware calendar, dated March 1989, hung on the wall. It displayed an antiquated photograph of downtown Prescott with crowded streets.

"Check out those old cars," Pete said, zeroing in on the picture. "This whole mansion is a time capsule."

"Yes, one with secrets," Suzanne said. "Bizarre."

"Whoever lived here took loving care of this place," Kathy said. She opened the ancient fridge door and hurriedly slammed it shut. "Yuck. There's still stuff in there!" A dreadful, stale smell flooded the kitchen. "What an awful odor!"

Pete loved bugging his sister. "What did you expect, flowers?"

"Who asked you?"

Time had extracted its toll. Ceiling and wall paint had blistered years before, dropping in patches. Wallpaper bubbled out in irregular shapes. Cobwebs hung in the corners.

The foursome separated into teams. Suzanne and Kathy wandered into the hall and toured the main floor—formal dining, living, family, and reading rooms, all boasting expensive, old-style furniture. The ten-foot-high ceilings were coffered with elaborate moldings and gilding. Whoever had decorated the home had spared no expense.

Solid wooden bookcases lined the walls of the library, stuffed with tomes of every size and description. Dozens more books littered the floor, tossed in haphazard piles.

"Check this out," Suzanne said. "The hunters have been here."

There were knickknacks and souvenirs arrayed across the shelves, including three two-by-three-inch gold picture frames, each featuring a calligraphed quotation. One read:

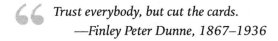
Trust everybody, but cut the cards.
—Finley Peter Dunne, 1867–1936

"That's what Dad says," Suzanne recalled.
"I've seen this one before," Kathy said, picking up a second gold frame:

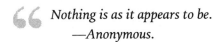
Nothing is as it appears to be.
—Anonymous.

The third quote made both girls laugh:

Neither man nor woman can be worth anything until they have discovered that they are fools.
—Lord Melbourne, 1779–1848

Artworks, torn from the walls and ripped from their frames, littered the dusty, carpeted floor. A piece of needlework read Home Sweet Home.

The library's cabinet doors were open, their contents rifled through, spilling onto the floors. "They turned this place upside down," Suzanne groused.

"They sure did," Kathy replied, pointing to the scattered books. "What on earth were they looking for?"

Meanwhile, upstairs the boys were conducting a methodical search of four large bedrooms and two bathrooms. In the master bedroom, two pillows lay together in the center of a king-size bed, its dusty sheets pulled aside, as if someone had just stepped out of bed. The mattress shifted off-kilter at a crazy angle.

In the three other bedrooms, the hunters had flipped over made-up mattresses, tilting them toward the floor. The ransacked dresser drawers and clothes closets were a mess, their contents spilled everywhere.

Tom knelt to touch a white dress with pastel colors running through it. "No dust. They haven't been here long."

The boys returned to the main level. "Anybody go downstairs?" Tom asked.

"We're on our way," his sister replied.

Natural light filtered through the basement windows despite the surrounding overgrown hedges. Cell phone flashlights lit up. The space seemed to be almost a perfect square and, like the rest of the house, huge. To their left and right, a handful of cardboard boxes lined both sides. But opposite the stairwell—stretching across the entire wall, floor to ceiling—appeared a mahogany bookcase.

"That's the largest bookshelf I've ever seen," Kathy said, taken aback. "But you can count the books on it with two hands."

"Well, sure. I mean, how many books could one couple own?" Suzanne said, trying to figure it out. "They jammed the main floor library full."

Instead, dozens of small cardboard storage boxes—folded shut on top, one after another—rested on the shelves in a neat and ordered fashion. The girls searched gently through a few at random, but nothing shed light on the mystery.

"Clothes, books, magazines, and old VHS videos," Suzanne muttered, "all the same." They returned each box to its original place.

"We don't want to tip the hunters off," Kathy said. "They haven't been down here."

"Yet. . . Suzanne replied, her eyes flashing. "But they will be."

At the center of the basement was a pool table, its balls randomly spread across the dusty green felt, two cues propped against one side, ready to play. The white cue ball waited for the next shot, which had never come. A billiard scoreboard memorialized the score: 22–29.

"Crazy," Suzanne said. She rolled the eight ball across the table, forging a path straight into a cobweb. "It hasn't moved in decades."

4

EUREKA!

At the center of the triple garage sat a dark blue two-door Ford. Except for a thick layer of dust, the stunning classic looked almost new.

"Whoa," Pete said, catching his breath. "An old Mustang Hatchback—my favorite car ever."

Tom couldn't believe his own eyes. "Parked here, deserted, all these years? Geez. What year is it?"

Pete bent toward the dusty rear license plate. "Well, it's got a 1987 plate. I'm thinking it was brand new."

Both doors were open, and so was the empty trunk. A new smell filled their nostrils—a mixture of oil and moisture.

Pete jumped into the driver's seat and read the odometer. "Only 6,325 miles. I've never seen one with mileage this low. Imagine taking this baby for a spin. It's a five-speed manual. Hey, the keys are in it." He turned the ignition. Dead.

Tom said, "I'll bet it would fire up with a new battery."

"You'd have to drain the gas tank," said Pete, sounding every bit the aspiring engineer he in fact was. He popped the hood. The car had a 5.0L V8 engine. "This sucker is hot."

Tom opened the glove compartment. "Check this out." The car's registration and insurance papers were sitting in a see-through plastic envelope, yellowed with age. "The owners, Nick and Joanne Maxim."

"*Okay*," Pete said with a whoop. "Got 'em."

They glanced in the backseat to discover a small pile of flyers, junk mail, two newspapers... even an unopened bill from the local telephone company.

"The couple's address is on everything."

Tom reached over and picked up the telephone bill. He slipped it into his shirt pocket. "Maybe we can learn something from this."

Tools and boxes of junk cluttered the left garage bay. The right bay sat empty, with a patch of old, dried oil on the floor.

"So it's obvious the Maxims owned a second car," Tom mused. "I wonder what happened to it?"

"Mr. and Mrs. Maxim," Pete wondered aloud, almost to himself. "Where on earth did you go?"

The girls had gravitated to the mansion's formal living room, where they hunched over an album of old photographs. "It's like someone took them yesterday," Kathy said. "Clean and colorful."

Dozens of pictures centered on one attractive couple, in their fifties, both with sandy hair and big smiles. They had traveled a lot: England, France, Germany, Australia. Page by page, the couple grew older as the years flew by.

Some photos had handwritten captions. A snapshot labeled *First trip to Monte Carlo* featured a view of the French Riviera. Another caption read *Introducing Nick and Joanne Maxim—August 2, 1987.*

"So they got married," Suzanne deduced. "Look how happy they were." Mr. and Mrs. Maxim stood, frozen in time, wearing huge smiles and waving to an unseen photographer.

"It's curious," Kathy said, looking over Suzanne's shoulder, trying to find the right words. "There are no children or other relatives. Just this couple, at home or traveling the world. But one other guy keeps popping up beside them."

THE SECRETS OF THE MYSTERIOUS MANSION

"You're right," Suzanne replied. "In England and Germany too. And they sure liked to gamble. The caption on this casino shot is Hong Kong, and here Mr. Maxim is at a card table in Las Vegas."

Another close-up appeared at the bottom of the page. The unknown man held five cards and smiled at the camera. A pleasant-looking guy with thinning hair, tanned and relaxed, he wore a short-sleeved polo shirt.

"The look on his face says, *Four of a kind*," Kathy quipped.

Suzanne turned the page. "Whoa! They took this photo in the mansion." The Maxims posed, arms resting on each other, smiling into the lens. Beside them was their friend.

Kathy stared at the picture. "Oh my word, Suzie. Not just here in the mansion. Here in the living room, sitting on this sofa. Right where we are!"

"Too spooky," Suzanne said. She looked around, seeing what *they* had seen, and shuddered instinctively. Then she reached for her cell phone and focused on the photo. *Click.*

The girls glanced up as Tom and Pete returned from the garage. Suzanne pointed to the handsome couple. "This was the home of Nick and Joanne Maxim. Here's a picture of them in October 1987."

"Yup, that matches the names on the car registration," Pete said. He filled the girls in on the find in the garage, "The best Mustang ever."

"So they even left their car behind," Suzanne said, puzzled. "I mean, something bad must have happened. *Seriously*. People don't just desert their house and vehicle and just… just *disappear*."

"They had two cars," Tom explained. "There's only one left."

"Well, no matter what, they aren't around now," Kathy said.

Pete nodded. "You're right. They'd be old enough to be our great-grandparents. Who's the other guy?"

"No clue yet," Suzanne said, looking over at Kathy. She sat cross-legged, absorbed in a second photo album. "Anything interesting?"

"Yeah." Kathy hesitated, her voice uncertain. "This might explain a few things. I'm trying to figure out what it all means."

"What is it?"

"Well... it's a scrapbook of newspaper clippings. They all focus on the same news story. The first one is from the *Arizona Republic* and dates to January nineteen eight-four."

She turned the album toward the others. The headline, in a large black font, read "Brazen Phoenix robbery, guard shot." Now Kathy had their attention. "I'll read it to you."

> "'Armed robbers who held up A & M Gold at closing time on Tuesday are still missing. After shooting a security guard, the robbers, disguised in clown headgear, escaped with $2.2 million in gold coins and bars, plus a smaller amount of silver. Police are looking for two male suspects driving a dark-colored, late-model Ford Mustang Hatchback. No one captured the license plate number. Police spokesman Lieutenant Trevor Browning described the robbery as a professional hit.'"

She stopped, looking at Pete with questioning eyes. "A Ford Mustang Hatchback?"

"Dark-colored?" Suzanne's eyebrows shot up.

Tom exchanged glances with Pete and let out a low whistle. But Pete was always dubious about any break in a case that seemed to come too easily. "It was a popular model," he said. "Lots of people had Mustangs."

"If you say so," Kathy said, rolling her eyes. She turned the scrapbook pages, one after another. The articles, placed in neat sections under yellowing sheets of plastic, came from a variety of newspapers.

"It's all the same story," she explained, "from the *L.A. Times* and the *Tucson Daily Star*. Listen to this one from January nineteen eighty-nine." Again, she read the article out loud:

> "'Today is the fifth anniversary of the Phoenix A & M Gold robbery. Police are no closer to solving the crime than they were five years ago. A & M Gold and its insurance company have offered a $100,000 reward for the return of $2.2 million in gold. Although local and state police have followed up multiple leads over the years, they have all proved futile. Police admit they've reached a dead end.'"

"Hey, another reward!" Pete hooted. "Like the case of the ghost in the county courthouse. *That's great.*"

"Listen to the last entry," Kathy said, her voice rising. "It's from the *Daily Pilot*, February nineteen eighty-nine: 'Phoenix City Police issued a statement this morning. Just over five years after the famous robbery of A & M Gold, they have identified and interviewed a primary suspect. The Prescott, Arizona man denies any involvement in the robbery or the shooting of the security guard. Detective Ted Slater, the officer in charge of the investigation, said that without additional proof no charges were forthcoming. To date, there is no sign of the missing $2.2 million in gold stolen in the infamous heist.'"

"Eureka!" Tom whistled, looking around at his friends. "You know what that means?"

"Sure," Kathy said. "It's an exclamation of triumph after a discovery."

"Very funny," Pete said, frowning at his sister. "It means our nighttime visitors are hunting for all that gold."

Tom grinned. "Funny, huh? More than a century ago, gold mining was a big deal in Yavapai County."

Suzanne laughed. "Well, it turns out there's another gold rush—and we're right in the middle of it!"

5

POINTERVILLE

"Imagine that—a mansion hidden in a forest and forgotten by time," the Chief said, shaking his head. "That's a first around here."

After returning from a day of discovery, the foursome had filled him in on the remarkable saga. The story of the A & M Gold robbery, and of the utter disappearance of the attractive couple who had owned the mansion, spilled out into the Jackson living room.

"Can you run a background check on Nick and Joanne Maxim?" Suzanne asked her father.

"Sure. I'll get Joe Ryan involved. He'll help." Detective Ryan had worked with the mystery searchers on the case of the ghost in the county courthouse. He was a favorite of the foursome—a person who people liked and trusted upon meeting him for the first time.

"Have you ever heard of the gold robbery?" Pete asked.

"No, I haven't." the Chief replied. "It was long before my time. But I do recall a story about some local resident implicated in a big heist in Phoenix. Still, I think it's obvious what the hunters want."

"Why are they looking now?" Kathy wondered aloud. "Why after all these years?"

"No clue. Perhaps they found evidence from the past. Or one of them caught a rumor. Or they stumbled upon the mansion and located the same scrapbooks you did. Once you discover who they are, the answers to your questions won't be far away."

Suzanne raised a point. "Nineteen eighty-nine was a long time ago. How can we find out what happened way back then?"

"Detective Ryan will make inquiries," the Chief replied. "Check newspaper archives too."

"What about the reward?" Pete asked, trying his best not to show too much interest. "Would the insurance company still be offering it today?"

"I assume so," the Chief said helpfully. "If the gold hasn't been found, the reward is likely active. Someone will want the yellow stuff back."

"One other thing," Tom said, handing an envelope to his father. "We found the Maxims' most recent telephone bill in the backseat of the Mustang."

The Chief opened it and scanned both sides of the single-page bill. "There are five long-distance collect calls on it."

"And they're all from the same number," Pete said.

"Yeah, I see that," the Chief said. "Area code 619."

"Well," Tom said, leaning toward, "that number is unassigned under that area code. We tried it."

"So we researched online," Kathy said. "Back in nineteen ninety-seven, they split 619 into two area codes. It seems the local population had expanded, and they needed more phone numbers. Then they reassigned a number of the old 619 exchanges."

"The new area code was 760," Tom explained. "If you call that old phone number today—but with the 760 area code—you reach the U.S. Penitentiary in Pointerville, California."

The Chief's eyebrows shot up in surprise. "You know what that is?"

"You bet," Pete said. "It's a high-security federal prison."

"Not just any prison," said the Chief. "It's famous—*notorious* might be a better word. *Maximum* security."

Suzanne summed up their research so far. "And we think one of them was the Maxims' buddy."

KNOWING ABOUT THE HARD, BUMPY RIDE WAS ONE THING —experiencing it in the backseat of a car was a whole different ballgame. It was close to midnight, Saturday

"This is a crazy road," Pete said, gripping his seat belt.

"Track," Suzanne corrected him.

"No kidding," Kathy said, hanging on for dear life.

Tom soon coasted the Chevy to a stop. "Okay. We walk from here."

It was another frosty night in north-central Arizona. Everyone had worn a parka and warm gloves. They opened the car doors and stepped out into the winter stillness. It was eleven forty.

Suzanne led the way along the twisting path, right to the top of the moonlit hill. The foursome found a spot at the highest level and sat down, scrunching together for warmth. It helped that there was no snow and little wind.

"Can you see the mansion?" Suzanne asked the Brunellis. She pointed toward the former home, shrouded in trees and darkness.

"Yes, for sure," Kathy replied. "There's a horizontal line running through the trees. Is that the roofline?"

"It is," Tom said. He pulled out a set of binoculars and passed it around. There wasn't much to see. The mansion appeared dark and distant.

"It does look mysterious," Kathy said.

"You bet it does," Suzanne said. "And strange things are happening there."

They sat in silence, fending off the nighttime cold. Occasionally, one or another of them stood and jumped up and down for warmth. Time ticked by in slow motion as midnight came and went. They shifted uncomfortably.

"Maybe he's a no show tonight," Pete said. Disappointment had crept into his voice.

"Too early to give up," Kathy said, her teeth chattering.

Minutes later, a beam of light flashed in the darkness.

"He's back!" Suzanne exclaimed. The four of them jumped to their feet.

"*They're* back," Pete corrected her. Two arrows of light were bouncing around inside the mansion.

"Now that *is* spooky," Kathy said. A shiver ran down her spine, but she no longer felt cold.

Tom held the binoculars up for a better view. "Those lights are coming from the basement windows."

"They're back because they haven't found the gold," Suzanne said.

"And they hadn't touched the lower level yet, I'd guess," Pete said. "At least, until now. I'll bet they're busy taking it apart."

They gazed in silence, captivated by what was happening in the mysterious mansion. The beams danced close to each other.

Five minutes slipped past before Pete floored them all. "We need to check those guys out."

Kathy shot him a stunned look. "Are you *nuts*? What if they're armed? If they don't get us, Mom and Dad will."

"I know that," he replied. "I'm not suggesting we *jump* on them —just observe them."

"You *are* nuts."

"You wait here, where it's nice and warm."

"Drop—dead."

"I'll go with Pete," Tom said.

"No you won't," Suzanne retorted.

6

THE HUNTERS

Pete raced down the hill and pivoted onto the rough path, heading straight toward the mysterious mansion. The others hurried behind in total silence.

"All or none," Suzanne had argued after a heated argument. They agreed.

The hike was a three-minute jaunt in pitch darkness. They soon reached the clearing, stopping at the tree line to catch their breath. Arrows of light—closer, brighter, and more powerful—arced around the basement at random. The threat felt real, almost physical, and downright *sinister*. But there was no going back. Not now.

"We grab their pictures, then get out of here—fast," Tom whispered in a hoarse voice that betrayed his nervousness. "Are we in agreement?" There was a soft murmur of assent.

Pete, impulsive and primed, was beside himself. *"Let's go."*

There were three sets of front-facing basement windows, all partially hidden by hedges and without curtains. The twins approached the closest window, Pete and Kathy slipped over to the third one. All four carried cell phones—muted, flash off, camera app ready.

They knelt to peek through the foliage.

Two hunters—*gold hunters*—cloaked in darkness and carrying lantern-style lights, were attacking the giant wall-to-wall bookshelf, systematically yanking out all the small cardboard boxes and random-looking curios and knickknacks. As the mystery searchers watched in rapt attention, the men ripped open boxes, one after another, dumping contents onto the basement floor. Clothes, books, magazines, old videos, and more tumbled out before the bouncing lantern light. The beam from one lantern caught a toothbrush falling to the floor, causing the two men to laugh inaudibly—an eerie scene like a silent movie viewed through a dirty prism. Then they rooted through the stuff, pushing everything aside, looking for—*what?* No way could those little boxes hold millions of dollars' worth of gold.

It wasn't possible to see the men's faces; they were nothing more than moving shadows. As they labored on the task at hand, random light beams would strike a windowpane, causing the young mystery searchers to shrink back.

By now, a sea of every imaginable item littered the basement floor beneath them. They paused, talking. One man waved his arms, seemingly in frustration. Then—for a split second—a beam of light lit up one man's face.

Click. Suzanne hissed, "Got him." She signaled the Brunellis with her hand. The twins nudged each other and backed off.

Kathy retreated, but Pete hesitated for another thirty seconds. He grabbed a second shot—*click*—then pulled away, rejoining the others at the edge of the clearing. Just inside the shelter of the pines.

"I got 'em *both*," he said, grinning in the night.

ON SUNDAY, SUZANNE AND PETE SHARED THE CAPTURED pics, messaging them back and forth with each other.

Both had caught the profile of the first hunter. Half his face was lit up, the other half in shadow. The two eerie shots, similar but taken from different angles, displayed a man of about fifty years of age with a thin, sallow countenance and tight lips. He wore an unusual expression—*Disturbing eyes,* Kathy texted the others. His hair was greasy and turning gray, and he needed a shave.

"He's a very unhappy-looking individual, if you ask me," Suzanne noted when the four had gathered at the Jacksons' house later that morning.

"I sure wouldn't want to run into him in the dark," Kathy agreed. "Or a deserted mansion."

Pete had captured the only image of the second man. Ten years younger in appearance than his companion, the man's prominent feature was a scar that ran down from his right eye, circling across his cheek and touching his upper lip. He wore eyeglasses, tiny, thin lenses in slender wireframes over small, beady eyes. His fleshy face had a blotchy red tone, and his receding hair was sparse. Tom described his look as "cruel, even dangerous."

Kathy shivered. "We need to avoid that guy too."

"They've been searching every night," Suzanne noted. "They're frustrated."

"Even more reason to avoid them."

Pete forwarded the shots to Detective Ryan, together with a brief explanation. He included the names of the mansion's former residents, Nick and Joanne Maxim.

Meanwhile, Suzanne called Heidi Hoover.

"You looked in the windows?" Heidi asked. She couldn't believe it. *"When the hunters were in there?* Wow, Suzie. You've got more guts than I do, that's for sure. Were they armed?"

Heidi always prompted a smile from Suzanne. The reporter was just that kind of person.

"Too dark to tell," Suzanne replied, "but we took photos."

"You're putting me on."

"Nope, we got 'em both."

"Hurrah! Send them over, will you?"

"Sure."

"What else?"

"Well," Suzanne said, "you were right. The mansion blew us away. Except for the mess those two guys left behind, it looks as if the Maxims walked out of there yesterday. That place is a time capsule."

"Told you. Who are the Maxims?"

"The former residents, Nick and Joanne Maxim."

"You know this, how?"

"Pictures, car registration, their name is everywhere," Suzanne said, "including on the mail in their last delivery."

"I need a picture."

"Yup, I've got one for you. It's on the way."

"Great, thanks. Anything else?"

"Yup. We know what they're looking for."

"Tell me."

Suzanne filled her in on the robbery at A & M Gold.

Heidi's voice exploded with excitement. "Wow, oh wow! They're after the gold, no doubt about it. This is one heck of a story. Are you going back to the mansion?"

"Yup, today in fact," Suzanne replied.

"Way to go. I love you guys. You're the best mystery searchers in town. Be careful."

After lunch, the foursome sprawled out in the Jackson's family room, discussing a shared concern: time was running out.

Pete summed up the obvious. "They've pretty well taken that house apart and found nothing. How much longer are they gonna hang around?"

"They *could* walk away, empty-handed, leaving the place in a mess," Kathy said.

"Good luck with that," Tom argued. "Gold is a powerful draw. I wonder who told them about it?"

Suzanne adjusted an ornament on the family Christmas tree. She felt a twinge of sadness that another joyous holiday season had come and gone—she loved this time of year. "Well, for sure they don't know where the gold is."

"That's a fact," Tom said. "But I actually think they're looking for something else."

"Like what, for instance?"

"Like instructions—or a map. Something that shows where the gold *is*!"

A shocked silence descended upon the room.

"Whoa," Pete said, breaking the spell. "That never crossed my mind. The gold might not even *be* in the mansion."

"That's intriguing," Kathy said.

"Quite literally," Suzanne said.

Tom nodded. "No way are they looking for gold bars in those cardboard boxes."

A light clicked on in Suzanne's mind. "So *that's* why they're turning everything upside down."

"Yup," Tom said. "The boxes gave it away."

"So did the books," Kathy said, "but I never connected the dots."

They all looked at one another. "Okay, so they could walk. How are we going to stop them?" Suzanne asked.

"I don't know, yet," Tom replied. "First things first. Detective Ryan is trying to trace the identities of the two men. It would help if we could get their license plate number. We'll hide in the forest tonight and watch for them."

"What if they don't show?" Pete asked.

"You have any doubt?" Suzanne asked, her eyebrows raised.

"I don't," Tom said. "They won't give up on all that gold—not yet, anyway. Heck, those guys would burn the house down before they let that happen."

"I hope you're kidding," Kathy said, cringing. Images of the palatial mansion played in her mind. She crossed her arms.

"I wish I were," Tom said. "That's one reason we've got to beat them to it."

"To what?" Suzanne asked.

"To the reward, of course," Pete said exultantly. "Okay, we'll grab their plate number. What else?"

"Well, I think we need to listen to them," Tom said, teasing.

Kathy gave him a sideways glance. "Now you're proposing we pop in and have a chat?"

Tom laughed out loud. "Hardly." He turned to his sister. "Suzie, you remember the listening device, the bug we discovered in the Yavapai Courthouse Museum?"

"Wait a sec," she replied, sitting straight up. "You're thinking of installing that bug inside the mansion?"

"Why not? Detective Ryan let us keep it as a souvenir. We tested it using my cell phone as the receiver. It worked great, remember?"

"Oh, yeah," Pete said, recalling the clean sound. "It transmitted for six city blocks."

Suzanne liked the idea. "We'd be much closer than that."

"We sure would," Tom said. "Let's install it today, long before the boys show up for work. We'll listen in on them. Could be interesting."

"They won't have a clue," Kathy said.

Tom grinned. "That's the idea."

7

SECRETS REVEALED

The tiny microphone was a technological marvel.

Tom and Suzanne had discovered the device in the county courthouse, hidden above a ceiling tile. Planted by thieves, it listened surreptitiously to the conversations of museum staff and the city police.

After the case had wound down, Detective Ryan surprised the four with a gift: the super bug, as he called it. "You all love technology, put it to work. It'll just sit in an evidence box for a few decades." He smiled. "The Chief gave his permission."

The first thing they did was test the device's range. It transmitted a clear signal for an amazing half mile. But the tiny microphone had a serious limitation—it picked up sound from up to six feet away, at best. Within the mansion, it was imperative to find a location where they felt sure the gold hunters would spend a significant amount of time. *But where?*

"There's no guarantee they'll search in only one room... or even a certain part of the house," Suzanne said.

"And what if just *one* guy appears?" Kathy added.

"Unless he talks to himself, we won't hear a thing," Pete said, chortling at the thought.

Sunday afternoon, the four friends stood in the mansion's basement. By daylight, it appeared even more chaotic than the previous night. The hunters had littered the linoleum floor with the contents from dozens of boxes pulled from the bookshelves.

"What a mess," Suzanne said disgustedly. "It's hard to believe. No point in hiding the bug here. There's nothing left to tear apart."

"They don't care about this beautiful house," Kathy said. "They only care about the gold."

"How do we know where they'll search next?" Suzanne wondered aloud.

"Ah, good question," her brother replied, expecting someone else to supply the answer. Silence. "Okay, we don't. They've turned the whole place apart."

Kathy disagreed. "They tossed dozens of the books onto the library floor. But there are a hundred more on the shelves. Even more."

"Good point, sis," Pete said.

"They'll scan the rest of them too," Suzanne said. "It's just a matter of time."

A minute later, standing in the dead quiet of the library, they recognized the next challenge. The ceiling was ten feet high and decorated with ornate plaster moldings. Unlike the county courthouse museum, there wasn't a dropped ceiling with removable panels.

Tom held the bug in his hand, complete with its new battery, ready to go. "Where can we hide it?" he asked rhetorically. The tiny device was a silver metallic cube, just one inch long on each side, including a miniature microphone that peeked out from a flat surface.

"Well, we sure can't stick it on one of these shelves," Pete said, stating the obvious. Bookcases lined three sides of the room.

"They didn't care about these books, did they," Suzanne said, glancing down at the random mess.

"No," Tom said, "but that gives me an idea." Forced smiles appeared. Tom's ideas were famous. Or infamous.

"Okay," his sister replied. "I'll bite."

"Well, they'll never look at the books they've already searched, will they?"

"Never," Kathy replied.

"So let's cut up one of them and hide the bug inside."

"Oh, we can't do that," Suzanne said with a frown. She loved books.

"Perfect," said Pete, heading out to the garage to find a utility knife.

It only took thirty minutes to install and test the bug. Upon completion, it lay hidden inside a thick recipe book and buried by three others—one of them left wide open, almost touching the all-but-invisible microphone peeking up from above the floor.

"Oh, man," Pete said, jumping up and rubbing his hands together. "I can't wait."

That same night, after eleven o'clock, they made their way back to the mysterious mansion. The first order of business was to drop Pete off in the forest, at the end of the mansion's access road. His job was to grab a shot of the gold hunters' license plate.

"See ya' later," he shouted as he jumped out of the car. Dressed for winter, Pete wore a dark, warm parka with a hood—he wanted to appear all but invisible—extra-warm fur-lined gloves, and thick boots. He had no illusions. It could be a long, cold wait.

"Message us when they show up!" his sister called out.

Suzanne flipped the Chevy around and returned to Route 69. Within minutes, she let Tom and Kathy off at the end of the trail before making her way back to the highway. She parked, waiting for Pete's alert. Meanwhile, Tom and Kathy trekked up the path and crested the top of the hill.

There was nothing to do but wait.

It was spooky in the forest—odd noises came and went. Pete

carried a small spray can of animal repellent. Just in case. The wind whistled through the treetops, gusting often but never quite reaching ground level. A full moon lit up the cloudless night.

Pete hid himself deep in the forest, far back from the road. He heard the vehicle long before seeing it. Whoever drove was in no hurry. The car's headlight beams cut into the night, rising and falling in a wavelike motion along the roadway. Then the vehicle pulled into the sheltering trees, its tires crushing over frozen ponderosa pine cones before grinding to a stop. The headlights died away. Voices spoke in hushed tones. Two doors slammed shut. The sound of footsteps disappeared into the distance.

A message went out: *They're in.* On top of the hill, Tom and Kathy glanced at each other. It was showtime.

Pete waited a couple minutes before stepping over to the vehicle. It was a newish Volvo sedan. He clicked on his cell phone light, sheltering it with both hands and peering into the windows. Nothing stood out. Then he trudged around to the rear of the car. It bore an Arizona license plate. *Click.* He backed off a few feet and turned on the auto-flash. *Click.* A blinding light burst and instantly faded.

Footsteps! Coming toward him. Did they see it? Where to hide? Pete dived under the Volvo and pulled himself forward. His heart beat hard. He watched, not moving a muscle, as someone approached the vehicle on its right side. Only the man's lower legs and his heavy, thick-soled work boots were visible. The passenger door opened. *They forgot something.*

The car squished down with the man's dead weight. Pete slid back a few inches, trying desperately not to make a sound, ready to scramble out. *And run as fast as I can!*

The man stepped out and slammed the door shut. He walked back toward the mansion, disappearing behind trees within seconds.

Pete waited another minute, his heart slowing, before pushing himself out from under the car. He hurried away, marching along in the gully beside the road, grateful—*so grateful*—that Suzanne hadn't appeared two minutes earlier. Meanwhile, Suzanne cruised toward him, headlights off, until Pete jumped out and flagged her.

THE SECRETS OF THE MYSTERIOUS MANSION

"I darn near ran you down!" she complained. Pete climbed into the front passenger seat, grinning. Suzanne pulled a sharp three-point turn before speeding into the night. He filled her in.

"Boy, you were lucky," was her only comment.

"And so were you."

Fifteen minutes later, Suzanne raced to the top of the hill, beating Pete by a few feet.

"Hey!" he called out. "You cheated!"

"Anything?" she asked the other two.

"Not a thing," Kathy replied. "We picked up voices but couldn't make out a word."

Pete gazed over at the mansion. Two flashlight beams bounced around inside. "They're upstairs!" he blurted out.

"Yup," Tom said. "We might be out of luck, at least for tonight."

"What the heck," Pete said. "We looked upstairs. They'd already turned the place upside down."

But a few minutes later, the flashlight beams moved down to the main floor. Tom held his cell phone up to his ear.

"Are you sure that bug is working?" Kathy asked, doubt creeping into her voice.

"Positive."

"Well, why can't we hear anything?"

"Because they're not in range," Pete replied, glaring at his sister in the dark. "Unless a mouse stomps over the mic, there aren't any other sounds for it to pick up."

"Who asked you?"

"You shouldn't—"

A metallic voice cut into the night air. "I'll take this bookcase, you take the other one." Crisp audio drove the foursome into silence. Books slammed onto the floor. Minutes passed before there was another word—a bad one. Then things got interesting.

"Maybe there's nothing here," a voice said.

An older-sounding man answered. "That's not what he told me."

"Might be a bunch of crap."

"I doubt it. That two-point-two million is real."

"You mean three-point-three million, don't you? Gold is up fifty percent in value since nineteen eighty-nine."

Someone chuckled. "Inflation is great, right?"

In the darkness, the four friends glanced at one another in astonishment. Tom whistled in a low tone. That thought hadn't occurred to them.

The younger voice spoke. "This isn't easy. No clue where to look."

The other man replied sharply. "All we know is that Paul said *he* would recognize it, whatever *it* is. If it's here, we'll find it. You want that gold, or not." It wasn't a question. Not the way he said it.

Over the next hour, there were bouts of silence, followed by earthy banter between the two men. Once, the younger-sounding man revealed the reason for the late-night searches.

"I wish that girl hadn't shown up. This midnight hunting is a drag."

"Well, she did. Nothing we can do about it."

"Heidi," Kathy said in a soft voice.

Later—much later—one man announced, "I give up." His voice sounded heavy and resigned. The flashlights clicked off.

"It's over," Tom said. "And the bug worked."

"Did it ever," Suzanne replied, giving her brother a high-five.

8

HIDDEN IDENTITIES

Early Monday morning, Suzanne's phone buzzed with an incoming message.

Gotta meet, when and where?

"It's Heidi," Suzanne said to her brother. "Something's up."

After lunch, the foursome headed off to the Shake Shop—their favorite go-to meeting place since junior high.

"Any hints?" Kathy asked.

"Nothing," Suzanne replied. "And she didn't return my phone calls either."

Heidi waited for them on an outside picnic bench. A thin folder rested on the table beside her.

"I hope you're ready for this," she said, as the foursome joined her. She opened the folder and pulled out two black-and-white copies of newspaper articles.

"Fatal Crash Claims Two," read the first headline. Suzanne's hand flew to her mouth. The group went silent for a few moments.

Kathy asked, "The Maxims?"

"I'm afraid so."

"When?"

"You won't believe this," Heidi replied. She paused, scanning their faces. "March twenty-first, nineteen eighty-nine."

"That's the same date as the newspaper on the kitchen table!" Pete exclaimed.

"Weird, huh?" said the reporter. "It explains a lot."

"How did it happen?" Tom asked.

"A semi slammed into them on 89A. It totaled the Maxims' Caddy. They both died at the scene."

"Oh, wow."

"So there's your missing car," Pete said, glancing at Tom.

"What's the second article?" Suzanne asked.

Heidi pulled the clipping out and slid it along the table. "It's a story about the funeral. They didn't hold it for ten days, which is unusual. Know why? The authorities were looking for next of kin—kids, relatives, anybody."

"Guess what?" She paused again, scanning their faces. "They couldn't find any. And no friends, either. In fact, the only couple who showed up were the ones who had sold them the mansion—a Mr. and Mrs. Russ Stevenson. Not another soul was present."

"So sad," Kathy said.

"Yeah," her brother said, "but they had at least *one* friend."

"You're not kidding," Suzanne agreed, looking at Heidi. "Remember that pic of the Maxims I sent over? There's a third person in the photo."

"Sure, I saw him," Heidi said. "The Maxims were hugging each other. He was the guy to the side."

"That's him," Kathy said. "He's in a couple dozen other pics with them. And over many years too."

"Including one shot in the living room of the mansion," Suzanne said, bringing the picture up on her cell phone. "Here he is again."

They all craned their necks for a better view. The Maxims and their friend were about the same age. He was a pleasant-looking fellow, tanned with light-colored, thinning hair, smiling and dressed in a short-sleeved polo shirt. "It's date-stamped," Heidi said. "Did you check it out?"

"No," Suzanne replied in surprise, glancing at Kathy. "We never even noticed." She enlarged the photo. It read: Sept 27, 1988.

"The authorities couldn't find the guy," Tom reminded.

"And we think we know why," Kathy said, explaining the connection to the penitentiary at Pointerville.

"Okay, I get it," Heidi said. "On the other hand, maybe he didn't *want* to be found. Like the Maxims, for instance."

Surprised, the four looked at her, trying to read her face.

"Wh-what on earth do you mean?" Kathy stammered.

"I'm guessing the Maxims never really existed," Heidi replied, closing the folder. "There's no trace of the couple before nineteen eighty-seven. No city records, no court records, no county info—with one exception."

"The mansion purchase," Pete guessed.

"Bingo. They bought it on August third, nineteen eighty-seven and wrote a check for the full amount. According to county records, they paid Russ and Hilda Stevenson eight hundred and forty-five thousand dollars."

Tom said, "In those days, that was big money."

"You bet it was," Heidi replied. "Huge. Russ Stevenson had built the palace in nineteen eighty-four."

A light clicked on in Kathy's mind. "Suzie, remember the picture in the photo album, the one on the beach we thought celebrated their wedding? Where it said, 'Introducing Nick and Joanne Maxim?'"

"Yes, I sure do."

"That wasn't their *wedding day*," Kathy said. Her eyes danced. "It was the day the couple became Nick and Joanne Maxim."

"*Of course*," Suzanne replied. "Before that, they were somebody else!"

"You bet they were," Pete said. "That makes total sense."

"Wow," Tom said, locking eyes with Kathy. "You hit that one right out of the ballpark."

"Most certainly did," Heidi chuckled. "Now you've got a mystery within a mystery." Her voice dropped and her eyes blazed. "That's always the best kind."

Just then, an unmarked police car pulled into the parking lot. "Hey, it's Detective Ryan," Tom said, surprised to see him.

Their favorite detective parked and made his way over to the picnic table. He carried a slim briefcase under one arm. "Hi, y'all!" he called out in his western drawl. "The Chief said you'd be here."

They all stood to greet him. "Have you met Heidi Hoover?" Suzanne asked.

"I have not," the investigator said, blinking as he extended his hand. He wore his trademark well-worn rumpled suit and glasses with lenses as thick as a Coke bottle. "But I've read your stories. It's a pleasure to meet you. Where do I order coffee?"

Once Detective Ryan had sat down, coffee in hand, the group backed up and debriefed him.

"Well, that's interesting," he said, "and it ties in with what I discovered—which isn't much. I couldn't find a thing about the Maxims until they bought that house. Before that, they didn't exist—not on paper, anyway, in this state at least."

"Exactly," Heidi agreed, nodding.

"Did you read the funeral story?" the detective asked.

Heidi replied. "Uh-huh. Got it right here."

"The couple were a pair of unknowns," the investigator said. "Why? Because they had no past."

"Then who are they, really?" Kathy asked.

"No clue yet," Detective Ryan replied. "But I've got a fingerprint team in the mansion this morning. Prints all over that place—I'm hoping we identify them within days."

The four grinned. Some of those prints belonged to them.

"People who create false identities have good reason to hide," Tom surmised.

"That's the way it is," the investigator replied. "And often because they're wanted by the law. I believe Mr. and Mrs. Maxim were hiding out in the forest. Perfect spot—their own special private prison."

"No nosy neighbors asking questions," Suzanne said.

"And no unexpected visitors either," Pete said.

"So they're tied into the gold robbery?" Tom asked.

"That would be my guess," the detective replied.

"Mine too," Heidi said. She chuckled. "And those gold hunters would agree too."

"That leads us to their identity," Detective Ryan said. He caught Pete's eye. "Thanks for sending over the license plate."

"You're welcome."

"Unfortunately, that plate isn't registered to anyone. We think it came off a junkyard car. So nothing there—at least for now. But you struck pay dirt with those two photos you sent over. The FBI's facial recognition database got hits."

Ryan retrieved two five-by-seven photographs from his briefcase, sliding one across the picnic table. It was a prison photograph with an identifying number at the bottom.

"That's our guy," Suzanne said. She recognized the sallow face, thin lips, and disturbing eyes. Unmistakable.

Pete agreed. "I'd recognize him anywhere."

"Who is he?" Kathy asked, gulping.

"His name is Harold 'Doc' Johnson," the investigator replied. "He served twenty-five years in Pointerville, a federal lockup in California, for a string of bank robberies. They released him ninety days ago."

Heidi and the foursome exchanged knowing looks.

Tom pulled out the telephone bill they discovered in the Mustang Hatchback and slid it across the table. "In the weeks before their accident, the Maxims accepted collect calls from the U.S. penitentiary in Pointerville."

"Five times," Kathy said.

"Oh, that's interesting," the detective said. He paused, zeroing in on the long-distance calls. "I wonder who they knew there."

"We're betting it's their friend in the pictures," Pete said.

"And I'm betting you're right," Heidi said. "No wonder he didn't show up for the funeral."

9

NAMES AND FACES

Detective Ryan frowned as he sipped his hot coffee. "This stuff tastes worse than the station brew." He pushed the cup away. "That explains a lot. Cons talk behind bars. Our two friends learned about the gold heist from inside—from someone familiar with the story. And they believed it."

"We picked up a name on the transmitter," Tom said, excited to report their technology had produced results. "A guy named Paul." He explained about the bug, and the conversation they had overheard.

That impressed the detective no end. After all, he had donated the super bug to the foursome. He smiled to himself. "Okay, Paul huh. That's helpful." The investigator paused. "I'll contact the prison—they'll tell me who Doc was chummy with. In the meantime, watch out. It's no fun tracking armed and dangerous criminals."

"Who's his buddy?" Tom asked.

The detective turned over the second photo and slid it across the table. "This gentleman is Jim 'Scarface' Wright. Prison authorities told me no one ever called him 'Scarface'—at least not to his face.

He picked the souvenir up in a prison fight ten years ago." Ryan took another sip of coffee and grimaced once more.

"What was he in for?" Tom asked.

"Gun smuggling across the border. He had a profitable operation going until the feds sent him up for ten years. He and Doc shared a cell for a time. His release was six months earlier. Mr. Wright needs to be careful. Doc Johnson has a habit of turning on his partners in crime."

The color in Suzanne's face drained away. "Oh, brother, just what we need. A couple more bad guys armed to the teeth."

ANOTHER BLUSTERY NIGHT FOUND THE FOURSOME BACK on the chilly hill. Monday's daytime sun had melted away much of the snow. Patches of white remained under the sheltering trees, glittering in the light of the almost-full moon, but the hillside itself was bare. The wind whistled.

Inside the mansion, a lantern clicked on. A second one followed moments later.

"They're back!" Tom yelled. He pulled out his cell phone and touched the transmitter app.

No one wanted to miss whatever happened next. Within minutes, the men were in the library once again, ripping out more books, fanning them open and tossing the rejects onto the expanding pile.

Tom cranked the volume up to the maximum level. With the wind noise, it wasn't easy to pick up every word.

Still, the gold hunters' conversation came through in spurts, interspersed by lengthy periods of silence. One exchange confirmed the names of the two partners in crime.

"Jim, check it out." A long pause followed.

"I don't think it's anything. Someone writing in the margin."

"I guess you're right. For a second…" The wind whipped up, obliterating the sound for a few moments.

"What about this, Doc?

"Nah."

The men's conversation became muffled and even more difficult to understand. "Almost impossible," Tom complained. "I bet I know why: they've buried the microphone under a heap of books."

"Oh, I get it," Kathy said. "That makes sense. We'll rescue it tomorrow."

An hour later, the flashlights went dark.

ON TUESDAY AFTERNOON, DETECTIVE RYAN CALLED JUST as the mystery searchers were about to head back to the mansion. "I've got news."

"You're on speaker," Suzanne said.

"We've got a hit on those fingerprints," the detective said. "We pulled a perfect set of prints belonging to a Mr. Lawrence Perreault. I've never heard of him, but back in the eighties he appeared on the FBI's Ten Most Wanted list."

"What did he do?" Tom asked.

"Bank robberies. Here in the U.S., Britain, and France. Born and raised in Paris and spoke multiple languages. Loved to gamble. Moved to America in nineteen seventy-seven and pulled off at least three major jobs on the East Coast—including a big jewelry heist in New York that netted him millions. The FBI told me he disappeared in nineteen eighty-five. Eventually, they dropped him from the list, figuring he must have died."

"They had that one right," Suzanne said.

"No wonder he liked to gamble," Kathy said. "He used other people's money."

"Stolen loot," Pete added.

Tom said, "So Perrault was Nick Maxim, and he pulled off the A & M Gold robbery."

"It sure looks that way," the detective agreed. He hesitated. "But there were *two* thieves responsible for that string of robberies on the

East Coast. And a team of *two* who robbed A & M Gold. Maxim—I mean, Perrault—had a partner, and that other guy *had* to know about Maxims' unfortunate accident."

Kathy said, "If the Maxims' death *was* an accident…"

"Yeah," Detective Ryan said, grunting. "That crossed my mind too. Could be Perrault's partner bumped him off to get the gold. There are two problems with that theory."

"His partner was behind bars," Pete said.

"And the gold hunters!" Suzanne said.

"Yeah, my thoughts too," the detective replied. "If someone had bumped them off, the gold would have disappeared."

"And therefore no hunters," Pete said.

"What about Joanne Maxim?" Tom wondered aloud. "Were you able to identify her?"

"Nope," Detective Ryan replied. "I'm sure we lifted her prints, but nothing pinged the database—here or in Europe. She took her real identity to her grave with her."

"Whoa," Kathy said. "That explains why no one showed up to their funerals."

Suzanne blanched. "Their families didn't even know they had died."

A FEW HOURS LATER, THE FOUR FRIENDS WALKED INTO the library to retrieve the bug. Tom was right: they found it buried under a heap of books. He moved the device back to the top of the pile and placed an open book tented over the tiny microphone.

"Is this still the best place?" Kathy asked. "They're darn near finished in here." It looked as if the two men had *almost* completed their ransacking. The books—piled high on the floor or tossed back onto the bookshelves in random fashion—had undergone close scrutiny.

"Well, let's check out the rest of the house," Tom suggested. "Maybe there's a better place we've overlooked."

THE SECRETS OF THE MYSTERIOUS MANSION

There wasn't. The bug stayed put.

10

BEEP, BEEP...

"We need to circle around the mansion," Pete urged. "Quick, before they shut down for the night."

The foursome stood on the chilly hill, focused on the sight across the way. It was New Year's Eve. Well, *past* that really... midnight had come and gone. They had hoped the hunters would take the night off, and that—after a little surveillance—they could join their families to celebrate.

"I mean, *come on*," Kathy had said earlier. "No one works on New Year's Eve!"

No such luck. And whatever the gold hunters were doing appeared to be different—much different than previous nights. They had arrived just after midnight and moved upstairs. Then they split up, searching the second-floor rooms. The curious thing was the time spent in every room.

"Nothing makes sense," Kathy argued. "They've been through all those rooms at least twice before."

"What's taking so long?" Suzanne asked.

"Pete's right," Tom said. "We need to check it out."

It should have been only a three-minute walk as the crow flies, but the circuitous route they took through the forest doubled the trek. Soon, they climbed a hill on the far side of the mansion, about two hundred yards distant, high enough to offer a clear second-story view.

Tom pulled out a set of binoculars and focused on the master bedroom. From time to time, beams of light arced across the tiny slices of dirty glass visible among the dense tangle of vines. Once, just for a moment, he caught an image of one man lit by his partner's flashlight: Doc.

Pete couldn't stand the uncertainty. "What's going on? What do you see?"

"Doc is in the master bedroom," Tom replied. "Other than that…"

Kathy asked, "What's he doing?"

A beam of light swept across the windows again. "I can't tell yet."

"Can I see?" Suzanne asked. Tom hesitated before passing the binoculars to his sister. Everyone fell silent.

Soon, Suzanne passed the binoculars to Kathy. Pete waited, so impatient he couldn't stand it.

"They carried a ladder in this time," Kathy said. "It appears as if one guy in heading into the attic."

Two minutes passed. "He's coming back down. Empty-handed."

"C'mon," Pete said, poking his sister. "It's my turn."

"Manners," she chided him before passing the binoculars.

Not much later, Pete raised an arm in the air. "I've got it!"

"What?" the others chorused.

"He held something overhead and his flashlight caught it," Pete said. "It's a *metal detector*."

"Of course!" Tom said, slapping his forehead. "Why didn't we think of that?"

"You're the 'idea guy,' hotshot," his sister said. "Why didn't *you* think of it?"

THE SECRETS OF THE MYSTERIOUS MANSION

Hall's Hardware rented metal detectors, but the business was closed on Wednesday, New Year's Day. The two families attended St. Francis Church together, followed by their customary brunch.

That night the gold hunters were a no-show.

"First night they missed," Pete said, disappointed.

"Too busy celebrating," Suzanne figured.

"Or recovering," Kathy joked.

First thing Thursday morning, the foursome rushed out and drove to a downtown still decorated with bright lights and giant Christmas ornaments. A beautiful nativity scene adorned one of the big windows at Hall's Hardware. Bells rang as they walked through the front door. A post-Christmas sale had brought in a good-size crowd.

"Look," Kathy said, "a forty percent discount on seasonal merchandise."

"Who—cares!" her brother protested.

Mr. Hall was an old friend of the twins' father. Plus, he had played an incidental role in their first adventure—the mystery on Apache Canyon Drive. They liked him.

Kathy pictured the two gold hunters in the mansion. "Hold it. You don't think *they* rented the metal detectors from Hall's Hardware, do you?"

Tom considered the idea. "That never crossed my mind."

Pete rolled his eyes. "Kathy, you think of the weirdest things."

Mr. Hall finished up with a customer and hurried over to say hello. The storekeeper wore a collared short-sleeve shirt and sported a small-brimmed straw hat that covered most of his white hair.

"Hi, you all," he said, greeting them with a smile, shaking hands. "Did you have a good Christmas? How can I help you?"

Soon, two metal detectors rested on the counter. Mr. Hall

provided a quick overview on how to best use them. "Very simple." Then he asked, "What are you doing, hunting for gold?"

Everyone laughed politely.

Kathy had triggered the question running in Tom's mind. "Mr. Hall, do you rent these often?"

"Not too much. But I sold two a few days ago."

"What?" Kathy exclaimed, turning toward the owner. "You *sold* two of them?"

"Yup. Sure did." He smiled.

"Any idea who the buyers were?" Tom asked.

"Not a clue. Two gents who paid cash."

Pete produced his cell phone and touched *Pictures*. "Were these the two buyers?"

Mr. Hall adjusted his glasses and angled the cell phone. Pete flipped back and forth between the images.

"That's them. Did they do something wrong?"

"Well, they're working on it," Tom replied, avoiding the question. "We're trying to figure out what they have in mind."

Pete glanced over at his sister with open admiration. "Kathy, you're a genius."

"I know it," she replied, tossing her head. Then she laughed.

On the way out to the mansion, a discussion centered on where to begin their search.

"They didn't find a thing upstairs," Suzanne said.

"That leaves us the main floor, garage, and basement," Kathy said.

"It makes no difference," Pete said.

Tom disagreed. "We should attack the basement first."

"Why?" Suzanne asked.

"There's something odd about it."

"Like what?"

"It's the wrong shape."

"What do you mean?" Kathy asked, puzzled.

"Well," Tom replied, "take the first floor, for example. It's a huge rectangle, right? I mean, the mansion's structure is basically a giant box, rectangular in shape."

"So is the second level," Pete said.

"Now consider the basement," Tom suggested.

A moment passed before Suzanne spoke up. "It's more like a square."

"That makes no sense," Pete admitted. "Good eye, Tom."

They arrived at the mansion after one in the afternoon and headed downstairs. The metal detectors were easy to use—even light enough to lift overhead and sweep across the ceiling—and they covered a range of a few feet. The closer they came to metal, the faster the units beeped.

And they beeped often. There were steel studs and copper piping inside the basement walls and steel under the concrete floor. The metal detectors were frustratingly sensitive. The contents of a few of the cardboard boxes, strewn in heaps across the basement floor, also contained bits of metal, which triggered the detectors.

"I'll have a giant headache before this is all over," Kathy complained.

Pete and Kathy searched every square foot along the east, west, and north walls, floors, and ceilings. Half an hour passed before they handed the metal detectors over to the twins.

Tom and Suzanne checked all the cabinets but soon reached the huge bookcase on the basement's south wall. They started on opposite sides. The two units went nuts.

Beep... beep... beep, beep, beep beep beepbeepbeepbeep they pinged, their insistent sounds coming faster all the time. The foursome glanced at one another as the twins ran the metal detectors across the entire bookcase.

"*Half* of this wall is pushing them to the max," Suzanne said. "What's back there?"

They shut the machines off. Total silence enveloped the room.

"There's something big behind this bookcase," Tom said, barely containing his excitement.

"Oh, boy," Suzanne said, eyes dancing. "This is like the ghost in the county courthouse case. There's a hidden entranceway here—maybe with a metal frame or doors."

"You bet there is," Kathy said. She was already tapping the shelves.

Soon the four of them were knocking, rapping, and even punching the individual shelves. *Nothing*. Next, they stripped everything away—boxes, books, curios, knickknacks, pencils, a pen, paper —in a very careful and systematic fashion, so they could restore all the contents to their original position. Every time they removed an item, they pushed and prodded the shelf surfaces and the bookcase's back wall, searching for some kind of trigger. Something. *Anything*.

They paused, frustrated and excited at the same time.

"If this bookcase is a false front, where would it open?" Pete asked.

"Who knows?" his sister replied. "The opening could be anywhere."

"A center opening would make sense," Tom said, running his hands over the solid wood.

Suzanne agreed. "The two center pieces stand out a bit from the rest of the bookcase. You're onto something."

Each of the bookcase's center sections was about five feet wide. They abutted each other, floor to ceiling, and protruded beyond the flanking sections by inches.

"Solid as the Rock of Gibraltar," Pete said.

The four of them pushed and prodded for another half hour before they found the "key." Or rather, before Suzanne discovered it. While sliding one hand across the surface, she pressed a tiny, inconspicuous six-inch-wide panel, recessed in the top left corner of the righthand center section, which slid to one side with an audible click.

"*Look!*" Suzanne whooped. The two center sections released, sliding sideways in opposite directions to reveal a central aperture. "All you have to do is push on a hidden 'key' and it opens!"

"That's all, huh," her brother said dryly.

"Wow, oh wow!" Kathy almost shouted.

Before them was the door to a gigantic, gleaming stainless-steel vault.

11

FALSE FLAG

The mystery searchers gasped in astonishment. Hands ran across the icy-smooth steel door, almost seven feet tall and four feet wide. A large five-spoked wheel extended from the surface at eye level, right beside a small black combination dial. A classic, giant, walk-in vault—the kind one would see in a bank—had materialized before them.

"I can't believe my own eyes," Suzanne said, breaking the silence.

"Oh, my goodness," Kathy said.

"How can we get into this monster?" Pete asked.

"Turns out you were right, Tom," his sister said. "The floor plan of the basement is a huge rectangle—*if* you include the vault."

"Yup, it figures—now it matches the rest of the house."

"That means this walk-in vault must be a decent size too."

"*The gold!*" Pete blurted out. He reached over and grasped the black dial with his fingertips. Soft, continuous audible clicks sounded as he spun the smooth circle. "We need that combination."

"Yes, for sure," Kathy said. "But right now we've got a bigger problem."

"What do you mean?" her brother asked.

"We have to stop the gold hunters from finding this vault," she replied.

"Ouch, good point," Tom said. "But how?"

They all glanced at one another.

Suzanne hesitated. "We could always lead them astray."

"*How?*"

"Well, leave a clue for them. That's what they're looking for, after all. Something that points the way to the gold...but leads them away from the mansion. We can manufacture a clue and hide it—some place where they're sure to find it."

"That's a great idea, sis," Tom said.

Pete said, "Kind of like a false flag. Devious. Very. I like it."

"Love it," Kathy said.

Pete considered their options. It was already after three o'clock in the afternoon. "We gotta work fast."

Using an old sheet of paper they found in the library, Suzanne wrote a note in pencil. It read:

> *Paul,*
> *The gold is in the cave one mile due north,*
> *the same one we found last year.*
> *Good luck.*

"Why not give them Google coordinates?" Kathy asked.

"Because there *was* no Google in nineteen eighty-nine!" her brother replied with a touch of sarcasm. He knew Kathy would get even later.

The foursome had chosen an imaginary location, one that wouldn't be easy to reach. "There's no road anywhere near," Suzanne said. "Nothing but rolling hills, rocks, and a few trees. And hopefully an old mine or two to keep them busy."

"Snakes too," Kathy reminded. She hated them.

Tom suggested they obtain a gold coin to "salt the mine"—the spot where they would hide their note. That way the metal detectors would react, allowing the hunters to discover the note. "Plus, the gold will show credibility."

"And send them on their merry way," Kathy giggled.

Suzanne wondered where they should hide it. "Has to be somewhere their metal detectors will sniff out."

"You figure it out," Pete suggested, glancing at his sister. "Dad's got an old gold coin."

"Oh, sure," Kathy said. "I remember it."

While Tom and Suzanne remained behind, the Brunellis raced home. Pete drove while Kathy called her father to ask if they could borrow his coin.

"Sure," he agreed. "It's in my dresser drawer. Do I get it back?"

A quick forty-five minutes later, the Brunellis returned, bouncing down into the basement.

"Did you find one?" Tom asked.

"Sure did," Kathy replied. "An old Mexican coin, about half an ounce of gold." She had looked it up online.

"Enough gold to set the metal detectors off?" Suzanne wondered.

"Let's try it," Pete said. He fired up one and moved it toward the gold coin, which Kathy held in her hand. The detector beeped like crazy within a radius of two feet. Cheers rang out.

"Where's the note going?" Kathy asked.

"Right here," Suzanne replied, pointing. Under the basement stairs were two smallish recessed built-in bookshelves, with four or five books resting on each. One book, titled *Prescott Seekers*, was a "how-to" primer on gold panning in the region.

The girls looked at each other and roared with laughter. "If all else fails…" Kathy joked.

It was obvious the gold hunters hadn't checked out these books—yet.

"But they will," Tom said. "Right after their metal detectors react."

Suzanne carefully folded the note and slid it inside the front cover of *Prescott Seekers*, with just a slender edge of the paper peeking out. She tucked the coin just behind the edge of the binding along the spine.

With the false clue planted, they slid the two center sections of the massive bookcase back together and meticulously restored its contents.

"Oh boy," Pete said, grinning. "I can't wait."

MIDNIGHT. THE FOUR FRIENDS WERE BACK ON THE HILL. They no longer had the advantage of the bug, which they had retrieved from the pile of books in the library, reasoning that the metal detectors would quickly expose it.

"If they found it, we could kiss the bug goodbye," Tom said.

"Not to mention, we'd alert those guys, big time," Suzanne said.

"I'll miss the sound of their voices," Kathy joked.

They agreed on something else too. If the two men worked the basement level, one sleuth had to act as a spy and surveil them.

"We need to watch them," Pete argued. "It's important that we see their reaction to the false flag. But it's way too dangerous for all four of us to tramp down there. I'll go alone."

Tom agreed. "Pete's right."

"Sure he is," Suzanne said. "Let's draw for it."

They drew lots, eliminating all but Kathy.

Half an hour later, the familiar lantern beams lit up the main floor of the mansion.

To their dismay, the mystery searchers—following the beams of light as they swept over the windows—observed the men heading straight for the garage. But ten minutes later, the lights reappeared, bouncing around the main level before disappearing into the basement.

Pete whooped. "It's a go!"

"Okay, Kathy, you're on," Tom urged. "Be careful. Keep your cell phone ready in case something comes up."

With a flippant "See ya!" Kathy whipped down the hill and sped along the now-familiar path. Her heart beat faster as she crossed into the clearing and approached a basement window. *Was it the exertion of the rush, or the fear of discovery?* she wondered. *Both,* she decided.

She edged up and peered down into the basement. In daylight Kathy would have enjoyed a clear view of the stairwell and both inset bookshelves. Now, darkness cloaked the basement level.

Two shadows worked along the wall, floor, and ceiling close to the stairwell. Each man carried a metal detector in one hand, holding it out at an angle, and a lantern-style flashlight in the other. They searched apart at some distance. Kathy caught the intermittent, muffled *beep, beep* of the detectors through the windows. Every so often the sound sped up before fading away. Once, she glimpsed the inset shelves, all the books still in place.

They haven't gone there, yet, she thought. But there wasn't long to wait.

The *beep, beep* of a detector turned into a continuous tone. One man was yanking books from the inset shelves. Moments later, they found the false flag. Kathy heard raised voices, still muffled, through the window. She picked up only isolated words and phrases.

"Look…" One hunter focused his lantern on the note as the gold coin fell to the floor.

"It's addressed to…" His voice dropped lower. Kathy moved closer to the window.

"Well, it's…" his partner replied. "One mile…?"

"Yeah, who would've…" A man's voice faded once again. Light reflected from the gold coin, nestled in one man's hand. As they talked, random lantern beams arced around the basement.

"*Hey!*" someone yelled.

Kathy shrank back, *too late!* The man had spotted her.

Gripped by panic, she raced away at high speed, losing her way among the ponderosa pines. Seconds were precious—*where to go?* Kathy had a good head start—her pursuers had to maneuver back up the stairs and out through the mansion's backdoor. But footsteps soon pounded along the ground behind her. Her mind raced. *Footprints*—there were still patches of snow under the trees. She could be easy prey—the thought made her giddy with fear. As she stumbled across a broad exposed outcropping of rocky ground swept clean of snow by the wind, Kathy had a brainwave.

I'll go straight up. They'll never see me. She reached up to grab a low-hanging tree limb.

Instead, there was a sudden cracking sound as the ground collapsed beneath her feet. She tumbled down, far down, into a black hole, flailing her arms before slamming into a heap of dirt.

Everything went dark.

12

LOST AND FOUND

Something was wrong—*seriously* wrong. Lantern beams appeared in the clearing, silhouetting two male figures and then bouncing at crazy angles as the men scurried into the forest.

"*They're onto her!*" Suzanne gasped.

Pete, grim-faced, his voice hollow, agreed. "Yeah, but they'll never find her in those trees. Kathy knows how to take care of herself."

"Are you nuts?" Suzanne was almost crying. "Have you forgotten that there's snow in the forest? You could track a squirrel through those woods with no problem—how easy would it be to follow human footprints?"

Pete scowled. He messaged his sister: *Where are you?* He stared at his phone, worried to death. Nothing. He sent another—no response.

He started down the hill. "I gotta find her."

"*We* have to find her," Suzanne said grimly, falling in behind him.

"For sure," Tom said. "Don't make a sound. They'll be on us in a heartbeat."

As they grew closer, the three of them spotted lantern beams—rising, falling, and weaving through the trees—on the way back to the mansion. Apparently, a ten-minute search had ended. It soon became obvious the gold hunters had disappeared into the basement and, moments later, headed out for their car. No sign of Kathy, only the sound of an ignition firing up in the distance.

"Okay, they're outta here," Tom said.

Even though any incoming messages would trigger his phone, Pete checked his cell often. He messaged for a third time.

As they reached the clearing, Pete roared *"Kathy!"* into the forest. *"Where are you?"*

They walked into the sea of ponderosa pines in front of the mansion, spreading out and calling her name, again and again. "Kathy! KATHY! *KATHY!*"

"One good thing," Suzanne said. "There's a lot less snow than I imagined."

Meanwhile, Kathy had a dream. In it, she played the role of a small child lost in a shopping mall. Weirdly enough, her brother was a teenager on a search for his sister. "Kathy!" he yelled. *"Kathy!"* His voice echoed along the mall's corridor, bouncing off the walls. She answered him, more than once too. But he couldn't seem to hear her voice and she didn't know why. It frightened her.

Then she awoke. The dream was so real that Pete still shouted, "Kathy, where are you?" *Where am I?* Seconds ticked by before everything began to register. *I fall into a well, or something. But I'm alive.* She moved her arms and legs. She ached all over, but nothing seemed broken.

"Pete!" she shouted back. *"Pete!"* No response. His voice faded.

Kathy—petrified of snakes her whole life—felt the ground around her. Carefully. It appeared she had fallen into a round shaft and onto the bedrock lying below. *A well?* Moonlight glinted off shiny mineral deposits in the walls of the shaft. How far down had she fallen? Twenty feet? It was hard to tell in the dark. Not too far— but impossible to climb out.

Kathy had landed on a pile of the earth that had given way beneath her and cushioned her fall. If she was lying at the bottom of a well, it wasn't particularly deep. Narrow, yes—*five feet wide at most,* she guessed. She touched the walls all around with ease. Broken flat planks of damp, smelly wood lay about her, and a good-size chunk rested across her legs. She kicked it off.

Kathy gasped as her hand touched her cell phone—the treasured Christmas gift. She picked it up, praying the thing still worked, and breathing a sigh of relief when it did. But her heart dropped when she read *No Signal* on the screen.

With some difficulty, she rose to her feet, quite unsteady and leaning against a wall for support. Her body hurt. All over. Nothing broken—but there would be bruises. She held her phone above her, as high as possible. The screen flickered once, twice, before Pete's three messages popped up. Her heart soared.

Kathy turned on the flashlight to discover the shaft wasn't a well at all. Rather, it appeared to be a mineshaft—maybe a test site that had failed, she thought. She pointed the light up and realized she had tumbled down about twelve feet. No snakes either, of course. It was wintertime. She grinned to herself, held the phone high and clicked on *Recent Call*.

Pete jumped for joy. "Kathy!" he shouted into his cell phone. "Where are you? You frightened us to death!" The twins rushed over to him.

"I fell into a mineshaft," his sister replied. "Be careful—I don't want you landing on me! Follow a straight-line path from the left front window at a right angle to the mansion... about twenty feet from the edge of the clearing."

"Thank God you're okay," Pete said. "You sound like you're calling inside from a fishbowl."

"Well, actually..." she replied.

Suzanne grabbed the phone. "Are you all right?"

"I think so. Sore for sure, but nothing seems broken and I'm standing up. I'll shine the flashlight straight up. It should hit the boughs of a tree above. I was trying to climb it when I fell. Where are the bad guys?"

A minute later, Kathy spotted three grinning faces looking down at her—a funny sight, really, illuminated by her light beam pointing up from the bottom of the shaft.

"Hi, there," her brother called down, mocking her gently. "No snakes with you, I hope?" Her aversion to the scaly creatures was family lore.

"Hi there yourself," she replied. She felt a little embarrassed but wasn't about to admit it. "Of course there aren't any snakes. What a silly thought. Get me out of here."

"We need a ladder," Tom said. "There's one in the garage." The two boys raced off.

"What happened?" Suzanne asked.

"The gold hunters spotted me through the window. I ran out here and reached up for a tree. Next thing I know, I woke up down here in the middle of a weird dream."

"So you headed up, not down," Suzanne said. A section of the wooden hatch remained intact at the top of the shaft. "No wonder. Appears like rotten wood covered the hole."

"Yup, there are pieces of it down here. I guess I put my weight on it and—*Pow!* Next thing I know I'm laying at the bottom of a mineshaft."

"That *was* a bad dream."

"Would be if it weren't true," Kathy said wryly. "I wonder how many more abandoned mineshafts there are out here?"

Soon enough, Kathy climbed over the rim and touched ground. The first thing she did was to give her brother the biggest hug ever. Then she repeated the gesture with her two best friends. She teared up.

It felt good to be alive.

13

THE DRONE

Tom placed an urgent call to Ray Huntley, president of the high school's technology club, early Friday morning. One week had zipped past since Heidi invited the twins on a ride into the unknown.

"Ray, can we borrow the drone?" Tom asked. "It's important." The compact, lightweight machine had been essential in solving the foursome's first case, the mystery on Apache Canyon Drive.

A surprised-sounding Ray replied, "It must *really* be important. It's not even eight a.m."

Half an hour later, the drone—tucked into the backseat of the Chevy—was resting between the Brunellis.

The plan soon unfolded. After drawing lots to decide their roles, the twins dropped the Brunellis off at the mysterious mansion. Pete and Kathy would spend the day searching for the next essential clue. With the startling discovery of the massive hidden vault, they knew just what that was.

"Something that reveals the combination," Kathy said, her eyes sparkling. She still felt sore—"I mean, *seriously*"—from the previous night's adventure. But very lucky.

"You bet," her brother agreed. "But think how tiny it could be.

Nothing but a set of random numbers scribbled—anywhere, on any surface, on the underside of a shelf, on any page in any book, on any small scrap of paper! How are we going to find it? How could *anyone* find it?"

It promised to be a perfect day for flying the drone—cloudless, blue skies, a slight breeze, and warmer temperatures than the previous week's.

"Great day for hiking," Suzanne said. "And I hope they do!"

"We'll know soon enough," her brother replied.

The twins turned off the highway at nine in the morning, cranking hard onto the track first discovered by Heidi. Suzanne drove in as far as possible before stopping. "End of the road."

Based on Kathy's eyewitness account from the day before, the gold hunters appeared to have swallowed the bait. If so, their search *had* to occur during daylight hours. The twins' job was to deploy the drone every hour, surveying the countryside a mile due north of the mansion. Meantime, they would keep an eye—a drone eye—on the old mining road, protecting the Brunellis.

"No unexpected visitors," Kathy had said when they outlined the plan. "I like that."

The twins readied the drone for flight. With a slight whirring sound, the aircraft lifted and soared away, climbing to one hundred feet in seconds. The onboard HD camera captured a live video stream. Suzanne, operating the controller—it was only her second time as pilot—could see everything onscreen.

Tom monitored the view from an app on his cell phone. "Camera's live, image is sharp."

Suzanne piloted the flying machine over to the mansion and followed the dirt road out to Route 69. "Quiet and empty." Then she steered the drone in a wide circle around the structure, about one mile in diameter.

For the first time the twins noticed another home tucked into the forest, a half mile west. A white pick-up stood parked in its driveway. "Neighbors," Suzanne said. "I didn't realize the Maxims had any."

The drone's maximum flight time was thirty minutes before recharging. Suzanne kept a sharp eye on the controller, careful to bring the drone home before it ran too low on power. Each flight required a recharge time of one hour, using an adapter that plugged into the Chevy's lighter port. Then they started over again, taking turns to pilot.

Nothing until the fourth flight, at one thirty.

"Someone's out there!" Tom exclaimed, zeroing in on two hikers. The drone was at its maximum-allowed height of four hundred feet —a FAA government rule. The figures were mere specks until he zoomed in closer.

"Yeah, I see them," Suzanne said. "Where did they come from? And where's their car?"

Tom piloted the drone lower by a hundred feet, keeping it well behind the two men, hoping they wouldn't notice the device. "I *think* the guy leading is Doc," he said. Then he pulled back, climbing up to the drone's maximum height once more. "Don't want them spotting it."

"Been there, done that," Suzanne said with a smile, recalling scary moments during their adventure on Apache Canyon Drive.

North of the mansion, the forest gave way to rolling country, rockier with a smattering of stands of trees.

"That's not an easy hike," Suzanne noted as one man lost his footing.

Tom steered the drone back toward home base. Soon they spotted a car parked on the side of a dirt road, close to where they had first seen the men. The flying machine swooped down and hovered behind the late-model Volvo, capturing its license plate number. Any remaining doubt of the hikers' identity vanished.

"What happens when they don't find a mineshaft or a cave?" Suzanne wondered aloud.

"When they come up empty," Tom replied, "their only option is to attack the mansion once more."

"I hope they don't figure out that we planted a false flag," his sister said.

"Impossible," Tom replied. "No way."

MEANWHILE, THE SEARCH IN THE MANSION CONTINUED unabated.

The Brunellis had spent most of the morning on the main floor, checking and rechecking every room. In the library, Kathy examined the remaining books still on the shelves. She opened each one, flipping through the pages before replacing it onto the shelf. *Nothing.* In the dead quiet space of the mansion, time dragged.

"I'm hungry," Pete complained.

"You're always hungry."

They gathered around a corner of the kitchen table and unpacked sandwiches. The foursome had packed in food and drinks for the afternoon. Afterward, the siblings moved downstairs to search for a clue—*anything.* They were on the floor, rooting through foot-deep debris, when a black Labrador retriever took them by surprise, racing down the stairs and circling them at high speed, its tongue hanging out and panting hard.

"What the heck—" Pete said.

"Well, hello there! Where did *you* come from?" Kathy said, laughing as she held a hand out. She loved dogs.

A voice came out of nowhere. "What on earth are you doing here?"

The Brunellis jumped to their feet. Standing halfway down the stairs and glaring at them was a man who looked to be in his late forties—tall, broad-shouldered, and fit. His eyes questioned them. He wore jeans, a jacket, and a peaked hunter's hat. And he carried a shotgun, pointed downward.

The black Lab stopped in front of the Brunellis, its tail wagging like crazy. Kathy bent down to pet her and received a sloppy kiss.

"Well, uh…" Pete stammered, his face turning red. "Well, you—"

"Why is this place torn up?" the man demanded. He glared at the siblings with an angry frown.

"*We* didn't do it," Kathy said forcefully, locking eyes him.

"Then who did?" he snapped. The man walked down a few stairs and stepped onto the basement floor. "What a mess. And who *are* you, anyway?"

"Oh, boy," Kathy said, looking to her brother for support. "How are we going to explain this?"

HALF AN HOUR LATER, THE BRUNELLIS AND ELLIOTT Stevenson—that was his name—sat in the living room, trading information. He had removed his hat and set it down on a side table. He ran his fingers through thinning hair. The friendly dog—Mr. Stevenson said she was ten years old and named Lacy—lay fast asleep at her master's feet.

In exchange for an explanation—the *whole* story, including the long-ago gold heist—Mr. Stevenson shared his extensive knowledge about the mysterious mansion. "My father, Russ, built this place in nineteen eighty-four. I was a kid watching it go up. We lived half a mile away, due west of here, in a much smaller house that Dad had also built—in fact, my wife and I live there today. Once Dad completed the mansion in eighty-six, our family moved in. My bedroom was upstairs, last one on the right. My sister was across the hall."

He paused, seemingly lost in his memories for a moment. "Dad's real estate business went south in 'eighty-seven. The economy had hit a bump, and everything dried up. He needed cash, so he listed this house on the market."

"One ad"—Mr. Stevenson waved his hand around—"in *The Daily Pilot*, and that brought Nick and Joanne Maxim to our door. And no one else. *I mean no one.* Who would pay seven hundred and forty-five thousand dollars to live in a forest, smack in the middle of nowhere? Back then, that was a pile of money."

Mr. Stevenson continued, his eyes narrowing. "Nice people. I met them, twice, and waved to them in passing a few times. Nick had emigrated from Belgium, he told us, while Joanne hailed from New York. He had a French accent. You couldn't help but like them."

"Wait," Kathy interrupted him, "I've got something to show you." She disappeared for a few moments and returned with the photo album. "Here they are."

"Yeah, that's them, all right," Mr. Stevenson said. He whistled to himself. "Just as I remember. Such a long time ago."

Pete asked, "Did you ever see the guy sitting beside them?"

Mr. Stevenson peered at the photo once more. "Not that I recall. But I was a kid."

"He appears in many of the pics," Kathy explained, flipping through the photos.

"Well, something unusual happened the day the Maxims showed up," Mr. Stevenson said. "Nick Maxim told my dad that he didn't want to get into a bidding war with anyone. He offered an additional hundred thousand dollars over the asking price if Dad would take it off the market. Right then, that day."

He grinned. "Dad couldn't *believe* it. He was desperate to sell. Of course, he agreed, and a week later the deal was closed. We moved back into our old house, which my mom preferred—she'd never wanted to move here in the first place. Said it was too big. A year and a half later, the Maxims were dead, killed in that terrible car accident. My parents claimed my sister and I were too young for a funeral, but they attended. I guess no one else showed up. No family, no friends, just Mom and Dad. I remember them coming home, quite shaken by the whole experience. My mother cried for days, but I could never figure out why. I mean, she hardly knew them."

"Who owns the mansion now?" Kathy wondered.

"Well, that's a legal question, and there's no easy answer," the man replied. "My wife and I inherited the land all around it, including the access road. But the lot and house itself belong to the survivors or inheritors of Nick and Joanne Maxim, whoever they might be—if there are any. Obviously, no one ever showed up and staked a claim. After listening to your story, now I know why."

"Wouldn't the county claim the property if there's no next of kin?" Kathy asked.

"Oh, sure, I would think so," Mr. Stevenson answered, blinking as he thought about it. "But remember, all of this occurred decades ago. My guess is that the title for this mansion lies forgotten in a dusty book at the county recorder's office. I'm willing to bet there isn't a soul in the world who remembers this place existed, or what happened to it."

"Until," he added, looking around the room, "your two gold hunters showed up."

14

A NEW PARTNER

Lacy awoke with a growl and jumped up, baring her teeth.
"We've got company," Mr. Stevenson said, looking uneasy. He picked up his shotgun and cradled it in the crook of one elbow. The back door opened and closed.

"Where are you guys?" Tom's voice rang out.

Kathy shouted, "We're in the living room!"

"They're our friends, Tom and Suzanne," Pete explained.

The twins bounced in but stopped in their tracks when they spotted a man sitting there—holding a shotgun. Pete and Kathy handled the introductions while Suzanne knelt to make friends with Lacy.

"Pleased to meet you, sir," Tom said. "So, you live close by?"

"I do," he replied. "Just half a mile over the hill."

"Oh, sure," Suzanne said. "We flew a drone out here. Your home is the only one around. There's a white pickup parked there."

"That's mine," Mr. Stevenson replied, apparently amused at the thought of a drone flying over the local countryside. "You flew over my place?"

The foursome explained the purpose of the drone and how they had used it with remarkable success to solve the mystery on Apache Canyon Drive.

"We were keeping an eye on the gold hunters," Tom said. "But they gave up and headed for their car."

"They traveled back in this direction, then turned away from the mansion," Suzanne added. "If not, we'd have called Pete and Kathy to get them out of here."

"But you didn't spot me," the older man said. "I guess a person walking through the forest is all but invisible."

"For sure," Tom agreed.

Suzanne asked, "Do you come here often?"

"Maybe once a month," he replied. "Lacy makes sure we walk every day, but there are many paths—including lots of abandoned mining trails. Since I retired a year ago, we've been exploring them all."

Pete asked, "If you don't mind my asking, sir, what did you do before retirement?"

"Oh, I was an Army Ranger."

"Wow," Kathy said, brightening. No wonder he looked so fit. "We're glad to have you on our side."

Mr. Stevenson laughed. "Well, I don't know how I can help, but I'll sure try. I'd like to stop these two guys before they do any more damage."

Suzanne popped a question. "What about the vault, Mr. Stevenson? Did your father install it as well?"

A puzzled look crossed his face. "Oh, you mean the *underground shelter*. It's behind that bookcase in the basement. The Maxims added the bookcase after they moved in. Dad built the shelter for the family. He was an early 'prepper'—someone who believed in the threat of imminent social and economic collapse. He stocked the shelter with food and water. Even made sure it had its own air supply. The shell is a vault he purchased from a bankrupt Prescott bank. Those were tough times."

Mr. Stevenson paused and shook his head. "The shelter hasn't crossed my mind in years. My father modified it—I don't recall exactly how." He smiled at the long-ago memory. "My sister and I played hide-and-seek in it."

"Any chance there's any surviving documentation?" Pete asked.

"Like the combination, for example?" Suzanne wondered out loud.

Mr. Stevenson chuckled. "After all this time? Nope, nothing." Then it dawned on him. "Is *that* what they're looking for?"

Tom nodded. "What they're *really* looking for, we're sure, is the gold. But finding the vault would move them a giant step closer."

"We were doing our best to lead them away from the mansion," Pete said. "To allow us time to figure things out ourselves—before they do. But they'll be back."

"That's for sure," Suzanne agreed. "We can't stop them."

"Hmm," Mr. Stevenson said. He scanned their faces. "That is a problem, isn't it?" The room fell silent before he spoke again. "We could block the mansion's access road."

"We could? How?" Tom asked.

"My wife and I own a couple hundred acres out here," the former Army Ranger explained. "There are multiple trails in and out of the property, and I've blocked some with barricades and No Trespassing signs. We don't want strangers wandering around out here. There's only one road leading to the mansion—it's an old mining road. We can barricade it, but there's no guarantee they'll pay attention."

That turned out to be the truth. A few minutes before midnight, the Brunellis hid in the forest. They parked their car in a safe, secluded spot and trekked back to a view of the turnoff. Kathy walked behind her brother at a slower pace, still sore from her recent adventure. Just after twelve o'clock, the Volvo pulled up and stopped short of the new barricade.

A wooden barricade blocked the road, side to side. In its center, facing toward the highway, was a sign that read: No Trespassing

—Trespassers will be prosecuted. And, beneath that: KEEP OUT. Mr. Stevenson had supplied an existing gate, transferring it from another road. With enthusiastic help from his new young friends, he dug postholes in the frozen ground on both sides of the road. Together, they installed the gate.

It took all of sixty seconds for the passengers to act. As the Brunellis watched in rapt attention, Scarface leaped out of the Volvo, smashed the frozen lock to bits with a hammer, and swung the gate aside. He jumped back into the front seat. Doc floored it to the mansion.

On their way, Kathy texted the twins. The Brunellis hurried to their car and, fifteen minutes later, made it to the top of the hill. Suzanne, seated alone, greeted them.

"Where's Tom?" Pete asked in surprise.

"Those guys are in the basement," Suzanne replied, checking out the scene with binoculars. "Tom hiked down to spy on them."

Around the same time, her brother crossed into the clearing. He knelt beside the nearest basement window and peered in, watching as two shadowy figures worked away on opposite sides of the space. As the metal detectors pinged, the men worked their way from the stairwell toward the bookcase.

It's only a matter of time, Tom thought.

The dark figures rested their metal detectors against the walls, searching the immense bookcase with their lantern beams. Ten minutes later, an explosion of muffled words rang out.

The gold hunters had hit pay dirt. Or at least they thought they had. Tom watched as the two sections of the bookcase slid open. The two beams of light revealed the gleaming, stainless-steel door. Even in the darkened basement, it was easy to see that the men were beside themselves. Arms waved in the air. Voices rose in pitch and volume.

"We found it!" Tom heard a loud voice cry.

"… the truth!"

"What…"

One man focused his lantern on the vault's black dial while his partner spun it around. The shorter figure tried to turn the wheel but to no avail.

Time seemed to stop. Doc and Scarface ran their hands across the steel door. A lengthy conversation in hushed tones ensued; Tom couldn't make out a word. *"Where is the combination?* That's what they're asking themselves," he muttered to himself.

Soon, the two men walked up the stairs to the main floor. Their flashlights clicked off. Tom heard the back door close.

He melted into the forest, listening for a few minutes until a car started in the distance. Then he turned back toward the hill.

Their elation, Tom knew, would be off the charts—but so would their frustration. No doubt they believed the gold was close, but the combination remained an elusive secret.

For Doc and Scarface—and for the four mystery searchers—the hunt was about to intensify.

15

REVELATIONS

"Tom, *wake up!*" Suzanne shook her brother, hard. "Detective Ryan wants to see us at the station."

Bleary-eyed from another late night, Tom sat up in bed and checked the time on his cell phone: 8:00 a.m. "*Now?* On Saturday morning?"

"Right now. I texted the Brunellis. They're waiting for us."

The twins each wolfed down a bowl of cereal before heading off. Half an hour later, the foursome walked through the double glass doors of police headquarters. Detective Ryan greeted them in the lobby and led the way to a conference room—a much larger one than they had used during their last visit. He carried a file folder.

He noticed their puffy faces and chuckled. "If you don't mind my saying, you're all looking a little tired this morning."

"You're not kidding," Kathy replied, stifling a yawn. "It was another late night."

Suzanne added, "But well worth it."

The Chief joined the meeting, nursing a cup of steaming hot coffee. The mystery searchers filled in the two men.

"So they located the vault, but they have the same problem we have," Pete concluded. "No combination."

"Tell me more about Mr. Stevenson," the detective asked.

"Well," Kathy said, "he lives just half a mile away. His father built the mansion back in the eighties, when Mr. Stevenson was a kid. His family lived there for a couple years."

"And he's got a wonderful black Lab named Lacy," Suzanne remarked. Labs were her favorite.

"It's odd how he showed up out of the blue," the Chief said.

"Oh, Dad, believe me, he's okay," Tom assured his father. The Chief, a cautious man, respected the judgement of his twins and their two best friends. "He even supplied that gate on zero notice, drove it over in his pickup to the road, and installed it. Made no difference, however."

Suzanne, always a good judge of character, nodded. "For sure. We like him a lot."

A uniformed officer stuck her head in the door. "Your call is coming in now, Detective Ryan."

"Okay, great, thank you," Ryan replied. He turned to the foursome. "The call is from Detective Bob Risi, with the Cold Case Division of the Phoenix Police Department. He's an old friend."

A desk phone rang. The investigator put the call on speakerphone.

"Good morning, Bob. We have a room full of people. Can you tell us what you found?"

"Sure can, and good morning, everyone. The detective who handled the A & M case, Ted Slater, died many years ago. I reviewed the file and his notes. He identified one prime suspect, a Mr. Nicholas Maxim, from Prescott, but there was no proof and no path to filing charges. The case is still on the books, unsolved."

Tom moved closer to the phone. "May I ask a question?"

"By all means," Detective Ryan replied. "Fire away."

"How did the Phoenix Police Department identify the suspect?" Tom asked.

"A telephone tip from Prescott," the Phoenix officer replied. "In the notes I see the name of Hilda Stevenson."

There was a collective gasp in the room. "Oh, my goodness!" Suzanne blurted. "That's Elliott Stevenson's *mother*."

"The Maxims coughed up an extra hundred grand for the mansion," Pete reminded everyone. "That must have seemed suspicious."

"Yup," Tom nodded. "And the Stevensons might have seen the dark-colored Mustang Hatchback too. That was the getaway car."

"No wonder she cried her eyes out for days," Kathy said, recalling Elliott's words. "The poor woman suffered from guilt. She must have thought her phone call had somehow hurt them."

"Any idea why Detective Slater figured Nick Maxim was the robber?" Pete asked.

"Yeah, a few things," the officer replied. "Mr. Maxim was evasive during questioning—his wife too. Nick Maxim refused to take a lie detector test, and he had a murky background. A note in the margin of one memo in the case file states, 'Can't find proof he ever existed previously. Same for his wife.' Plus, the detective noted the Mustang Hatchback you mentioned. Hilda Stevenson drew his attention to it. The file says the vehicle never left the garage."

Kathy wondered what had happened to the injured guard. "Did he survive?"

The officer went quiet for a moment. Papers rustled in the background. "Yes, he did. It says here that he was back to work within a month."

The call wrapped up a few minutes later.

"Okay," Detective Ryan said. "I think it's obvious that Lawrence Perrault and Paul Schubert pulled off the gold robbery in Phoenix. Let's talk about Mr. Schubert."

The investigator opened the folder on his desk. He fingered a close-up photograph and laid it on the table. It was a headshot of a prison inmate. A number appeared at the bottom of the photo. "Recognize him?"

Everyone craned their necks to get a good look. "It's the Maxims' friend!" Suzanne exclaimed.

Kathy agreed. "You bet it is. He matches the shots we found in the photo album. Who is he?"

"Who *was* he," the detective corrected. "No one has a clue. The FBI arrested him in nineteen eighty-nine, just months before the Maxims died in the car accident. So your assumption was right. He had to be the individual who called collect from Pointerville."

A half smile crossed his face. It was clearly an interesting case. "The man used the name Paul Schubert, but all his identification proved to be phony. There was no such person, and his fingerprints failed to identify him. Mr. Schubert—whoever he was—died fifteen years ago behind bars at Pointerville. He never revealed his true name to anyone, so far as we know—which is unusual, to say the least. He was serving twenty-five years to life for multiple New York bank robberies. Plus they got him on that jewelry robbery that netted them millions, but he never ratted out his accomplice. Now we've identified his partner in crime."

"Nick Maxim, aka Lawrence Perrault," Tom intoned.

"Yes," the detective replied with a grin. "The FBI couldn't identify the second robber. But now, thanks to you, we can."

"Wow. Paul Schubert refused to talk," Pete said. "Ever."

Tom whistled. "Heidi sure stumbled onto something big this time. *Huge.*"

"She did," Detective Ryan said. He paused, allowing everything to sink in. "And here's the kicker: Harold 'Doc' Johnson shared a cell with Paul Schubert seventeen years ago—for about six months. Paul must have talked during one of those long, lonely nights in prison. I'm guessing he told Doc about the heist, the gold, and the mansion."

The Chief spoke up. "So that's how your gold hunters heard about the story. Paul Schubert knew about the vault, but there's no way he—or anyone else—had access to the combination."

"Nick Maxim told Paul about the combination... that it was somewhere in the mansion and provided a clue to where to find it," Suzanne said. "Something he, Paul, would recognize."

"During one of those collect calls," Kathy said.

The investigator nodded in agreement. "There's no doubt in my mind. Nick Maxim must have assured Paul that his share of the loot was safe, waiting until his release."

The team recalled the conversation they had overheard in the library.

"Doc Johnson said there was a *clue* hidden in the mansion," Pete said. "But he sure wasn't aware of the vault."

"You're right," the investigator said. "Paul must have kept that fact to himself—and he had no concern about someone else finding it, either. Years later, Jim Wright and Doc Johnson shared a cell before their release. Doc got out a month ago—Jim Wright six months earlier." His eyes narrowed. "Even after all those years, Doc remembered."

"'*Trust everybody, but cut the cards,*'" the Chief said. "An old-time gambler's maxim. No wonder they tore the place up. If these guys don't strike gold, they're bound to turn desperate. Be careful."

"We will," Suzanne assured her father. A murmur of assent rose around the table.

"The gold hunters said Paul would have recognized the clue," Tom said. "Perhaps something from his past or related to his interests."

"We know little about him," the detective admitted. "Except that he was an armed robber, and a successful one at that. But his identity will never surface. He took it with him to the grave."

"Well, one thing is for sure," Suzanne said, recalling the photo album snapshots. "He loved to gamble."

A light clicked on in Kathy's mind.

16

A DOOR OPENS

That afternoon, on the trip to the mansion, Suzanne called Heidi and put her on speaker.

"We've got—news!" she told the reporter. Heidi had a great sense of humor.

They filled her in on the latest events—about their meeting with Elliott Stevenson, the gate added to the mansion's access road, and the update from Detective Ryan. For the first time, Heidi heard about the discovery of the moving bookcase and the immense, stainless-steel vault.

"Man, oh, man, this case gets better by the day," Heidi chortled. "You'll find the gold, not a shred of doubt. Elliot Stevenson. Is he related to Russ and Hilda Stevenson?"

"Sure is," Suzanne replied. "Their only son."

"He was a little kid when his father built the mansion."

"Now he and his wife live in a house half a mile to the west."

"Elliott's mother tipped off the Phoenix Police Department," Pete said. "That's how they got onto Nick Maxim."

Kathy's face registered a huge frown. She wasn't at all pleased that her brother had revealed the secret. "We don't want to mention that again," she admonished him. "Ever. It makes no difference now."

"Just saying," he protested.

"Mrs. Stevenson was heartsick after the Maxims died," Kathy explained to the reporter.

"Don't worry, it'll never appear in the story," Heidi assured her. "This case has more twists than the path to the mansion. When are you guys going back out?"

"We're on our way!" Suzanne called out in the background.

"Listen," Heidi replied. "I'm stuck here for the next hour, but I'll join you as soon as I can. If you find stuff, don't move it before I get a pic. *Especially that gold!*"

An hour later, the Chevy was nosing into the forest, as close as the foursome could get to the mysterious mansion. Even before the car came to a complete stop, Kathy was out and bounding toward the clearing. She had a hunch that she couldn't wait to pursue. The others hurried behind her. Together, they ducked into the back door and headed straight for the library.

"There it is!" Kathy said. The three two-by-three-inch frames sat in a row on a bookshelf, each displaying its own proverb, undisturbed. They hadn't moved since the girls had spotted them a few days earlier. And before that, probably not for decades.

"'*Trust everybody but cut the cards.*'" The Chief's words, spoken that morning, rang out in Kathy's mind. That was the clue, and it made perfect sense. A dedicated gambler like Paul Schubert would have immediately recognized the famous old saying, hidden in plain sight.

As the others gathered around, Kathy grabbed the frame and flipped it over in her hands. Four tiny clasps held the frame and the glass to their velvet-covered stand-up backing. She twisted each clasp and pulled the backing away. A folded bit of paper fluttered to the floor.

"Look!" Kathy cried, kneeling to pick up the sliver of paper, brittle and yellowed with age.

Suzanne glanced at it and whooped. "The combination!"

Kathy read the numbers out loud. "Fifty-two, twenty-eight, forty-four, fifteen, thirty-one."

"Let's go!" Pete yelled. He whipped down the stairs.

"You found it," Tom said, locking eyes with Kathy. "You open it."

She turned and descended into the basement, proud, smiling, and taking her time. Suzanne had already opened the bookcase.

Kathy edged up to the stainless-steel door. She ran her hand across its cold, smooth, almost satiny finish, glancing at the combination again. She closed her eyes to regain her composure. "Left or right first?" she asked.

"Try left."

She spun the black dial in alternating circles. Nothing.

"Go right," Suzanne suggested.

Kathy did. Still nothing. A concerned look crossed her face.

"Calm down," her brother encouraged her. "You're just keyed up. Do it again and take it easy. Be sure to hit each number precisely."

Kathy closed her eyes and took a deep breath. Then she tried for a third time… before there was an audible, wonderful click. She gasped. Tom grabbed the circular wheel and spun it. The wheel stopped, and the door eased open a few inches.

"You did it!" Pete yelled. "Stand back."

Tom grasped the door and swung it wide, revealing an almost empty room—a dark space close to ten feet wide by fifteen feet long. *Almost* empty, because in its center rested a large black valise. Everyone stood motionless for a few seconds before rushing in.

Pete clicked on his cell phone flashlight. He reached down to touch the gold-colored latches on the valise. "There are two locks on it." Then he tried lifting the case. "Oh, man. This thing is heavy." It wouldn't budge.

"A few million dollars' worth of gold *would* be heavy," Kathy quipped. "What did you expect?" High-fives circled around.

"I can't believe it," Suzanne whispered to herself.

Kathy closed her eyes again. "That reward is ours."

"Not quite," a deep voice spoke from nowhere.

The foursome whirled around in shock. Two men stood behind them—*the gold hunters*. The older man, Doc, held a handgun pointed straight at them.

Warnings flashed through the four friends' minds. *They could be armed*, Heidi had said. *Dangerous*, the Chief had reminded them. And Detective Ryan: *Watch out!*

"What do you want?" Tom asked. His normally steady voice shook. He hoped the men didn't notice.

"Move to the back," Doc ordered. "All of you. And I mean now! Get in there." He waved his gun in the air.

The foursome backed up as a unit, moving closer together for protection.

"So, you're the ones who sent us on that wild goose chase," the younger man grumbled. The ugly scar running down the side of his face flared red with anger. Scarface had earned his nickname. "We wasted a day tripping around wild country—thanks to you."

No one responded.

"Sure, it's them," Doc said with a soundless laugh. "They were trying to keep us away—from this." He pointed toward the valise. "And one of these pretty little girls is who you spotted in the window."

Scarface's beady little eyes, filled with suspicion, bored in on Suzanne, then Kathy. "Oh, sure, you're right." He pointed toward Kathy. His scar flared again.

She shrank back, nudging closer to her brother. An instinctive shudder ran through her.

"So," Scarface said, "whadda we do with 'em?"

The men exchanged glances. The captives didn't move, their breathing still and quiet.

"We'll lock them in the vault," Doc said, spitting out the words. He glared at them—hard. "Who are you, anyway? And who told you about the gold?"

"A newspaper reporter we know stumbled across the mansion,"

Tom replied, shrugging his shoulders, hoping he had squelched the fear in his voice.

"We put two and two together," Suzanne added, trying to support her brother.

"Oh, sure, I get it," Scarface said. As his face twisted when he talked, the scar moved around—a creepy effect. "That woman who walked in the mansion." He glanced at Doc. "When I was here by myself."

"Doesn't matter. In your case, two and two adds up to zero," Doc said, pointing at them with his left index finger. "We win, you lose. Grab the case, Jim."

Scarface bent down and grabbed the handles. "I can't move it!" he wailed. "It's way too heavy."

"You grab one side, I'll get the other," Doc barked. With some effort, the men slid the valise along the steel floor and right out into the basement.

Doc straightened up and stared at the nervous group in front of him. His face registered a thought. "Your phones. I want them all. Just slide them along the floor." Four phones propelled toward the gold hunters. Scarface picked them up, tossing each one into the mess in the basement.

"Well, it's been nice meeting you. You all have a wonderful time in there!" Doc said, sneering.

A burst of laughter echoed before the heavy steel door shut tight. There was a *whoosh* sound, followed by an audible click. The four captives could sense the wheel turning. Utter darkness enveloped them, together with an eerie feeling of profound emptiness.

"Hilarious," Tom said dryly.

Not another word was spoken until Suzanne broke the silence. "Oh—boy. Now what?"

"Now we're cooked," Kathy conceded.

"Not true. Remember what Mr. Stevenson said," Pete recalled. "This place has its own air supply."

"Well, that's something," Suzanne said.

"You bet it is," Tom said with relief. "And we're alive and well."

"I wish we had our phones," said Kathy.

"They wouldn't work anyway," Tom said. "We're surrounded by steel."

Pete grimaced in the dark. "Kiss the reward goodbye."

"Where's Heidi when you need her?" Kathy quipped.

17

RESCUE

Heidi's braked hard, bringing her car to a sudden halt. Something was amiss. There were *two* vehicles parked at the end of the mining road.

One of them was the twins' white Chevy. The other was a late-model Volvo sedan. "Who else would be here?" she wondered aloud.

Heidi backed up and pulled into the forest, hiding her vehicle amongst the trees. She jumped out and ran toward the path. Noises ahead forced her to duck behind a stand of ponderosa pine—just in time. Two men, bent over and carrying a heavy load, were making their way in the opposite direction—cursing, complaining, and gasping for breath.

"Shut up!" one of them snapped. "You won't complain when we cash in."

"Yeah, yeah," the other man muttered. "This thing weighs a *ton*."

Heidi held her breath until they had labored by and were out of sight. She hurried into the clearing and darted around the mansion. Then she ducked through the back door, onto the landing.

"Tom, Suzie, it's Heidi! Where are you?" Silence greeted her.

She searched every room on the main floor and stepped into the garage, calling their names. "Pete! Kathy!" *Nothing*. Then she raced downstairs. Her eyes went straight to the immense bookcase. It was just as Suzanne had described—wall to wall and floor to ceiling—closed tight. Behind it, she had said, was a stainless-steel door.

"Hey, where are you guys?" she called out again. More silence. Heidi strode over to the bookcase and tried prying open the protruding center sections. It was hopeless. She backed away before noticing four cell phones tossed onto the floor.

She bent down and picked one up, turning it over in her hands. "Something's wrong," she said out loud.

Suzanne had told her about Elliott Stevenson. He lived close by, she said, half a mile away—due west. Heidi ran back to her car. The Volvo had gone. She headed out to Route 69 and chose the turnoff to the next road west. Five minutes later, she brought her vehicle to a hard stop in Elliott Stevenson's driveway. Moments later, Mr. and Mrs. Stevenson—together with the ever-enthusiastic Lacy—raced back to the mansion.

"How much oxygen would they have?" Heidi asked, worried as she glanced at the man in her rearview mirror.

"Not an issue," Mr. Stevenson replied. "The shelter has a hidden pipe leading outside. Air flows in. You think they're okay?"

"I sure hope so."

Heidi and the Stevensons soon circled the mansion with Lacy racing ahead, her tongue hanging out. Elliott stopped at the back of the house.

Knowing about the pipe and finding it decades after last seeing it were two different things. "I thought it was right here," Elliott said. He pointed to a spot on the exterior siding. "I remember it being circular and small, but where…"

The three of them searched for the next few minutes, even pulling ivy away from the mansion walls and burrowing behind the overgrown hedges. *Nothing*.

As time slipped by, Mr. Stevenson grew concerned. "I wonder if they might have installed new siding and covered the pipe," he said.

"Wouldn't you know if they had?" Heidi asked. Her voice was a little shaky. The man didn't answer.

"What about the side of the house?" Mrs. Stevenson asked. "Should we try there?"

"Nah, it's back here, I swear it."

His wife stepped around the corner. A minute later, she returned, pointing to the side and inquiring in a sweet voice, "Is this it, dear?"

"Aargh," Elliott complained. A one-inch diameter metal ring, covered in fine dirt-encrusted mesh, was built into the side exterior wall at waist-level.

Mr. Stevenson bent over and yelled into the pipe. "Hey! Can you hear me?"

Down below, in the darkness, the four friends, sitting on the floor with their backs to the steel walls, leaped to their feet.

"We can hear you!" they chorused. A wave of relief washed over them.

"It's Elliott Stevenson!" a man called back. Distorted by its twisting route through the metal air pipe, his voice was unrecognizable. "I need the combination!"

"Yes!" Kathy bellowed. "Fifty-two—twenty-eight—forty-four—fifteen—thirty-one!"

Elliott Stevenson repeated the numbers. Then he hurried downstairs, Lacy leading, with Heidi and his wife hot on his heels.

Elliott stared at the bookcase. "Any idea how to get in there?"

"Not a clue," Heidi replied. "I'll ask them." She whipped back to the pipe aperture for instructions.

A few minutes dragged by. The four stood—impatient, expectant, and overjoyed—inside. A loud, audible click brought a cheer to their lips. With a turning of the wheel, the vault door swung wide open.

Lacy squeezed in first. "Wow!" Kathy cried, giving the dog a big hug. "Am I ever glad to see you!"

High-fives cascaded around the room. Mr. Stevenson introduced his wife, Marlene—a demure lady who looked to be a few years older than her husband, tall like him, with long speckled-grey hair. Heidi received hugs but brushed off her young friends' expressions of gratitude. Mr. Stevenson graciously accepted a big thank you from each of the four.

"Where's the gold?" Heidi asked, ever the reporter.

Tom eyed his cell phone on the floor. He picked it and touched his father's emergency number. The Chief answered on the first ring.

"It's a crime scene now," his father said. His relief flooded over Tom's cell phone. "Thank God you're okay. I'll advise Detective Ryan, but you're not in our jurisdiction. I'll call the sheriff now."

Sheriff Steve McClennan of Yavapai County was a lifelong family friend. The mystery searchers had worked with him on the Apache Canyon Drive mystery. Twenty minutes later, he arrived, followed by the Chief and Detective Ryan.

For a crime scene, there wasn't much to process.

"So," Sheriff McClennan said after a brief meeting, "these guys swiped the gold that came from a heist—decades ago. Interesting. It's Christmastime for the insurance company, I guess."

"Provided we find the gold," Kathy said.

The sheriff chuckled. "Meantime, I'll charge these two gentlemen with armed robbery and unlawful confinement. Wait until the parole board gets the news. I'm guessing the thieves just bought themselves a one-way ticket back to Pointerville. We'll issue an all-points bulletin. Do we have their license plate number?"

Soon, everyone headed to their cars. Heidi and her friends drove over to the Stevensons' house, where Marlene hosted them for sandwiches and lemonade. The couple was fun to be around. Amid the laughter were a few somber moments—the Maxims' fate weighed on them all, even though it had befallen decades earlier.

By prior agreement, the foursome kept the identity of the long-ago tipster a secret. They had discussed Hilda Stevenson's call at great length earlier in the week.

"Hilda had a reason why she placed that call," Suzanne had said, making her case. "And she was right too."

Pete agreed. "You know, she could have remained anonymous. It's interesting that she revealed her name."

"We'll never know her reasons," Kathy said, commiserating, "but it's obvious that she paid the price."

Suzanne agreed. "The poor woman suffered. Let's let it go."

They did.

Later, before leaving, Pete handed his cell phone number to Elliott and Marlene, as the couple insisted that their new young friends call them. "Just in case," he said. "You never know."

YOU NEVER KNOW. PETE'S CELL PHONE, RESTING ON HIS bedside table, rang just after midnight on Sunday morning, waking him from a deep, exhausted sleep. He couldn't believe it. *Must be Tom,* he thought.

"Hello."

"Pete, it's Elliott Stevenson," he said, his voice muffled. In the background was a rustling sound. "Sorry to call you so late."

"No problem, Mr. Stevenson. What's wrong?"

"I couldn't sleep and took Lacy for a walk. There are lights flashing around the mansion."

Pete sat up in bed. "*Lights*? What the heck. Who's out there now?"

"I dunno," he answered. "But I'm walking over. I'll wait for you at the end of the road."

"Okay," Pete replied, jumping out of bed. "See ya soon." He raced into Kathy's room and shook her awake. Kathy messaged Suzanne—who replied seconds later: *On our way.*

It took the twins all of three minutes to dress and leap into the Chevy. Suzanne was at the wheel. Tom called the sheriff's office and reported the unexpected intrusion. It couldn't be the gold hunters, could it? They had scored and were on the run. Who else would be out there now?

Soon, their two vehicles met along Route 69 and turned onto the old mining road. The gate was still there, swung aside. The mystery searchers raced to the end, lights off, and parked side by side. There was no reason to hide their cars. Those days were past.

Elliott Stevenson appeared from out of the darkness. The former Army Ranger cradled his shotgun. "Two men, and they're in the basement," he said in a low, controlled voice as Lacy ran circles.

"Let's go see," Pete said, rubbing his hands together.

The five of them walked along the path and into the clearing. They made their way to the basement windows and peeked inside. Sure enough, random beams of light arced around the space.

"But we can't see them," Pete advised in a low voice. "Know why? They're in the *vault*."

"Must be quite a shock," Kathy mused, "seeing those empty shelves."

Tom huddled the group together in a circle. "We'd better hide in the trees. Deputies are on their way."

"Okay," Suzanne said, her heart beating faster. "We'll see who jumps out when they appear."

They trooped to the edge of the forest, fifty feet away. Each took a position behind a tree, eyes glued to the back door. A siren wailed in the distance, increasing in volume with every passing second.

"Oh, boy," Pete said. "Here we go!" He couldn't hide his excitement.

Another minute slipped past. The deputy turned onto the dirt road, his cruiser's emergency lights casting an eerie blue circle through the screen of trees. The screaming siren rose one last time before dying away.

"Here they come!" Tom cried in a hoarse voice.

Out of the mansion popped two shadowy masculine figures, ducking through the back door in the darkness, beelining their way to the trees at high speed—straight toward the hidden group.

The bigger man didn't see a thing—especially not Mr. Stevenson's right hook. *Never mess with an Army Ranger,* Kathy thought. The next second, the man lay flat on the forest floor, out cold. Lacy greeted the other man, barking her head off and leaping at him. He turned, shocked and disoriented, just as Suzanne slid out one flexed foot and tripped him. Her three friends pounced, pinning him to the ground, too surprised to defend himself.

Pete stood up and clicked on his cell phone's flashlight, aiming it at one man and then the other. Elliott Stevenson threatened them with his shotgun.

Suzanne looked down in disbelief. "Harold 'Doc' Johnson—and Jim 'Scarface' Wright!" she said. "What on *earth* are you doing back here?"

18

MOTHER LODE

The crime scene at the mysterious mansion had turned into a circus. Two deputies arrived, one after another, followed by Sheriff McLennan. After a 1:00 a.m. wake-up call from the sheriff, the Chief and Detective Ryan rushed to the scene.

All worries about the fate of the four mystery searchers soon evaporated. Elliott Stevenson had handled things well—"With a little help from my buddy," he chuckled, stroking Lacy.

Minutes later Elliott's wife, Marlene, drove over, attracted by a never-ending stream of headlights on the old mining road. "I always feel safe when my husband is nearby," she said.

The Chief thanked Mr. Stevenson, shaking his hand. "We owe you a debt of gratitude, sir."

"Oh, not at all," the man replied. "I was in the right place. Those kids handled themselves well. You should be proud of them."

Deputies soon bundled Doc and Scarface off to the county jail.

"They're a blight on society," Kathy joked, happy to see them go.

"We need to find their Volvo," Pete urged. Detective Ryan and the two boys backtracked to the access road and walked deeper into the forest. Five minutes later Tom yelled out, "Bingo!"

They found the car unlocked. The detective pushed the trunk

release button on the left side of the dashboard. Pete stepped to the back.

"The valise!" he shouted. *"Unlocked!"*

Inside, stacked tightly and filling the suitcase, were dozens of silver ingots, each one stamped with a seal specifying its purity and weight—ONE HUNDRED OUNCES—but no gold.

"That explains it," Tom said, putting things together. "They came back because they didn't get the gold—instead, they grabbed a case full of silver."

Pete wondered, "Silver's still valuable, right?"

"Sure, but not like gold. Not even close."

"Well, this thing weighs a couple hundred pounds or more, and it's all silver. How much is it worth?"

Detective Ryan guessed fifty grand.

Tom launched Google on his phone and did a quick search. "About fifty-five grand, at today's silver price," he replied.

"Man, oh, man," Pete exclaimed. "No wonder they came back. That's nothing compared to three-point-three million bucks in gold!"

"That means the gold is still nearby," Detective Ryan said. The man showed no emotion.

"Okay, that makes sense. But where?" Suzanne said when Ryan and the boys had returned. The vault was empty.

"Maybe it's not in the mansion at all," Pete suggested.

"Or," Kathy said, thinking out loud, "maybe it *was* there, but someone else already grabbed it."

"I doubt it," Tom replied. "Would a thief leave the silver behind?"

"Not likely," Detective Ryan replied. "Kathy, where did you find the combination?"

"In the library," she replied, "hidden in the back of a tiny picture frame."

"Is there anything similar still there?"

"Yes!" Suzanne replied first. She turned around and rushed up the stairs and into the library with everyone following behind. *It's so obvious,* she thought. Right in front of their noses the whole time.

She picked up another frame displaying a famous proverb. It had sat on the same shelf, right beside the first one.

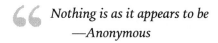
Nothing is as it appears to be
—Anonymous

THE FRAMES WERE IDENTICAL. SHE TWISTED THE FOUR tiny clasps on the backing and stripped it away. To her delight, a slim, one-inch-square piece of paper lay beneath. She turned the brittle bit of paper with neat, tiny writing over in her hand.

"A woman wrote this," Suzanne said. She read it out loud. "'Paul—The back wall of the vault is false. Push on it at eye level and stand away. Love, Lawrence and Barbara.'"

"Oh, my goodness," Kathy exclaimed. "The silver was a deliberate false flag."

"You bet it was," Tom said. "The valise was bait, and we fell for it. So did our gold-hunting friends."

"Who's Barbara?" Suzanne asked.

Pete tore out of the room, raced downstairs, and sprang into the vault, touching his cell phone flashlight at the same time. Everyone followed. He raised his hand, palm out. "Stand back!" He pushed the wall at eye level and heard a soft click. They all watched in stunned silence as a four-foot wide middle section of steel slid sideways with a slow, quiet, gliding motion.

"Must be a hydraulic mechanism," Tom said.

"Yup," Pete agreed. "And it still works great after all these years." More flashlights lit up.

"Look at that!" Kathy murmured. Behind the hidden pocket door were four deep shelves about six feet wide, all loaded with stacks of gold ingots, gold coins, and cash—in fifties and hundreds—too many to count.

Oohs and *aahs* broke the silence.

"The mother lode," Tom said, stunned. "That's what three-and-a-half million bucks looks like."

"More or less," the Chief said.

"You know who's gonna be the happiest?" Pete asked.

"It won't be those two bad guys," Kathy quipped.

"The insurance company," Suzanne replied. "They must have written all this stuff off years ago."

"Not only that," Detective Ryan said, "but they covered the value of the stolen gold—to the tune of two-point-two million dollars. In effect, they *bought* the gold, lost or not, at that price by paying off the policy. Their investment has soared in the meantime. Yeah, they'll celebrate."

Tom said, "That phone call will be fun to make."

"You should make it," his father said. "The four of you solved the case."

"We had a little help from our new buddy, Elliott," Pete said.

"Not to mention Heidi," Suzanne said. "*Who* is Barbara?"

The detective paused, stroking his chin. "Well, I think it's obvious that Nick and Joanne Maxim are the same as Lawrence and Barbara Perrault. We'll try to locate a marriage certificate for the couple, but it's a long shot."

"We know they lived in Arizona, New York, and France," Tom said. "There could be other locations too."

"You bet there could," Suzanne said. "Those two moved around."

"What if you can't find a marriage certificate?" Kathy asked.

The Chief replied. "Then we'll never identify Joanne Maxim for sure. She went to the grave under an assumed name. No one will ever know."

"That's the saddest thing I've ever heard," Kathy said.

19

BEYOND THE GRAVE

Christmas break ended. It was the fastest season ever, the four friends said later—and one they would remember for the rest of their lives.

On Monday morning, they eagerly returned to Prescott High, a school they loved.

"Timing is everything," Kathy said.

"You bet," Suzanne agreed. "We wrapped that mystery up just in time."

Still, there was one loose thread.

After school that day, the four hurried off to police headquarters for a pre-scheduled conference call. It was time to deliver the news to an insurance company based in Los Angeles.

The company's president, Scott Parker, couldn't believe it. "Let me get this straight. You're telling me you've recovered *all* the gold from the A & M heist?"

Kathy, the appointed spokeswoman for the group, replied. "Well, we're still counting, sir, but it sure looks that way."

Detective Ryan jumped into the conversation. "Based on our preliminary count, I think the answer is yes. We found a large amount of silver and cash too."

Mr. Parker didn't skip a beat. "You realize that heist took place in nineteen eight-four, right?"

"Yes, sir."

"I wasn't even out of grade school," the company president chuckled. "Where did you find it?" He still sounded incredulous.

Over the thirty minutes, the story spilled out. At one stage, Mr. Jackson mentioned the substantial increase in the gold's value.

"It's up fifty percent," he declared. "Even accounting for inflation, you can imagine the response from my board of directors."

Detective Ryan asked, "We assume the hundred-thousand-dollar reward is still active?"

"You bet it is," Mr. Jackson's voice crackled over the speakerphone. "Please provide the names of the recipients, with their Social Security numbers and banking details. I'll send over all the official paperwork for the transfer."

He thanked everyone again, for the third time, before disconnecting.

"We'll include Heidi Hoover and Elliott Stevenson on the windfall," Suzanne said. The four had discussed the reward on Sunday.

"And you, Detective Ryan," Tom said.

"Not this time," the detective protested. He held his hands up. "My role was marginal. Thanks, anyway. But I agree with you. The other two players were invaluable."

SATURDAY MORNING, A MEETING OCCURRED AT THE mysterious mansion.

"Forget *mysterious*," Kathy said. "Far from it, now. It's more like coming home!"

The invitation list included Heidi Hoover, Elliott and Marlene Stevenson, Detective Ryan, and the Brunelli and Jackson parents. And Sheriff McClennan, of course. The end of the access road soon resembled a parking lot. The Stevensons arrived first. Heidi rushed in minutes later.

THE SECRETS OF THE MYSTERIOUS MANSION

Elliott worked in the basement, packing piles of clothing and books into the discarded cardboard boxes. On the main floor, Marlene was busy restoring the library to its original condition. She even had a vacuum cleaner ready to go.

The four mystery searchers introduced everyone, then toured the mansion with their parents. The palatial home was a hit. So was the almost-new Mustang Hatchback. The hidden stainless-steel vault got rave reviews.

"Thank the good Lord that Heidi came along," the twins' mother, Sherri, said as she walked into the dark and chilly enclosure.

Both moms gave the newspaper reporter big hugs, despite Heidi's best efforts to fend them off.

They all admired Marlene, a quiet, thoughtful person, and polite too. "Have you ever seen such a mess?" she asked.

"We'll help today and come back tomorrow," Suzanne reassured her.

"Me too," Heidi offered. "We'll get this place shipshape in no time." They all signed up.

"Oh, wonderful," Marlene exclaimed. "I can't thank you enough."

Detective Ryan walked to the top of the stairwell and called Elliott into the library. Everyone gathered around, sitting or standing.

"Well, Mr. Stevenson," Suzanne began, "the insurance company has agreed to pay the original reward of one hundred thousand dollars for the return of the gold and silver. We wanted to thank you."

"Oh, no problem," he replied, his face turning color. "Happy to help. And please, my name is Elliott."

Tom said, "They need your address and Social Security number, plus a checking account number, so they can arrange a wire transfer. One-sixth of the reward is coming to you."

Shocked, Elliott stammered, "Th-there's no need for that."

"Yes, there is, sir," Pete said. "Without you, the recovery wouldn't have been possible."

Elliott received a big hug from his wife.

"In fact," Kathy joked, "without you, Heidi wouldn't have recovered *us*!"

Laughter rippled around the room. Applause broke out, led by the young investigators' four parents.

"We're very grateful to both of you," the Chief said, shaking hands with Elliott and his wife.

"They need your information too, Heidi," Kathy said. "One-sixth of the reward is also yours."

"How much is that?" she asked.

"It comes out to $16,666.66," Tom said.

"Who gets the extra four cents?" Heidi asked with a straight face. More laughter rang out. "Thank you. That's very generous of you."

"No sweat," Pete said. "You turned us on to the mysterious mansion. We wouldn't be here without you."

"That's a fact," Suzanne concurred.

Detective Ryan and Sheriff McClennan commended them all.

"Imagine what would have happened if even one of you hadn't stepped up," the detective said.

The sheriff added, "You're all heroes."

Everyone dug in to aid the Stevenson's clean-up project, working in each room of the house. Sherri and Maria attacked the bedrooms upstairs while Elliott continued his work in the basement. Marlene, Kathy, and Suzanne remained in the library, picking up books and picture frames from the floor and restoring them to the bookshelves and walls.

The boys worked in the garage. They even dusted off the Mustang Hatchback.

"Man, this thing is brand new," Pete said in an admiring tone. He couldn't get over it. The dark-blue muscle car gleamed.

Even the three police officers pitched in.

At some point the third tiny frame caught Kathy's attention. Its inscription read:

Neither man nor woman can be worth anything until they have discovered that they are fools.
—Lord Melbourne, 1779–1848

"Why not?" she whispered to herself. Deep in thought, she turned the frame over in her hands. Identical to the other two frames, it had four silver clasps attached to the backing of the frame. She twisted the metal clasps and removed the backing.

"Another note!" Kathy's hands trembled with anticipation. Suzanne and Marlene looked on in disbelief.

"Whatever could it say?" Marlene asked.

Kathy lifted the note from its cell. Then she called everyone back to the library. She held a slip of paper in one hand and the framed quotation in the other.

"Look what I found," she said, her voice subdued.

"You're—kidding," Tom said. "A third note?"

"What does it say?" Detective Ryan asked.

Pete said, "The quote says a lot by itself."

Kathy's eyes never left the scrap of paper. Like the other two notes, it was yellow and brittle with age. She read it out loud:

> "'Paul—We are so sorry they caught you. It was our fault for not meeting you on time. They won't release you for many years, and we're powerless to help. Now we are prisoners in this forsaken forest. There's nowhere to go, nothing to do. If you read this, you'll know where your share is. We were all fools. Your best friends, Lawrence and Barbara.'"

Seconds ticked by before the Chief spoke. "Wow. That's quite an admission."

"So many secrets," Suzanne said, holding her hand to her mouth.

"And so much regret." A tear rolled down Maria's cheek. "All for nothing. My heart goes out to them. I hope they had made peace with God before the end."

"A little wisdom from beyond the grave," Tom said. "The mysterious mansion had it all."

EPILOGUE

Pete's cell phone rang in the final quarter of Monday night football. He answered, his eyes never leaving the screen. It was third down, bottom of the fourth. The Arizona Cardinals were up and leading by a field goal. Kathy was as excited as her brother.

"Hello."

"Hey, Pete, it's Elliott Stevenson."

"Hi, Elliott," Pete replied, surprised to hear his voice. "How are you doing?"

"I'm great, but I think I've got something for you and Kathy."

Pete put him on speaker. "What's that?"

"First, let me ask you: Are you still driving your mom's car?"

"Yeah—when we can," Kathy jumped in. "Hi, Elliott. Sometimes we get Dad's car when Mom is at work."

"Do you need a ride?" Pete asked.

"No, no," Elliott chuckled. Marlene's laughter pealed in the background. "Here's the thing. I know that the Jackson twins have their own car, and you don't. How would you like to be the proud owners of a nineteen eighty-seven Ford Mustang Hatchback with less than sixty-four hundred miles?"

The siblings glanced at each other with quizzical looks.

Pete rolled his eyes. *If only.* "Well, Elliott, we're a little short of funds right now. That classic is worth a ton of money."

"Oh, we're not trying to *sell* it to you," Elliott said, chuckling once more. "If you need a car, we'd like to *give* it to you."

"Elliott, you—you gotta be kidding!" Pete stammered.

Kathy's arms went straight up. "Hooray!"

Marlene got on the line. "Well, the car's ready to go. Elliott had the title transferred already—it's in the mail. He installed a new battery and gassed it up. We don't need another vehicle, so it's all yours."

"I changed the oil too," Elliott said. "This car is like brand new."

Surprised and excited beyond words, the Brunelli siblings thanked the Stevensons more than once. Then they high-fived each other and called the Jacksons to share the news. The twins were busy taking down the tree and storing the ornaments.

They were just as pleased as their best friends.

"Awesome," said Suzanne. "I can't wait."

"Pete, a *Mustang Hatchback*. That's your favorite car!" Tom exclaimed. "What a gift."

"Half of it is mine!" Kathy shouted, rejoicing.

"We're still in shock," Pete said.

"We'll give you a ride out there after school tomorrow," Suzanne said.

Kathy got in the last word. "Once again, crime pays—but only if you're on the *right* side of the law."

EXCERPT FROM BOOK 4

THE HOUSE ON CEMETERY HILL

Chapter 1
A Stranger Arrives

"He *died*? He's dead? Whatever do you mean, Mrs. McPherson?"

Suzanne stared at the woman, dumbfounded. To judge from her hands, she had to be in her seventies. But you'd never have known it from looking at her face—or her style. She wore jeans, sneakers, and a sleeveless top. Her alert, bright eyes darted around the room. Short bleached-blond hair and a facelift—or two?—gave her a younger appearance, but her perfume was *way* too strong.

Suzanne shot a glance at her brother. Nothing the older woman had said made any sense. *Not even close.*

The drama had begun at nine fifteen that morning, right after the twins' parents left for the grocery store. While Tom struggled to get out of bed, Suzanne was brushing her long, auburn hair into a ponytail. The doorbell rang. She bolted downstairs and opened the front door, expecting to see Pete and Kathy. *They're very early*, it occurred to her.

EXCERPT FROM BOOK 4

Instead, a tiny older lady stood outside, her nose pressed against the screen. Suzanne, tall and willowy like her brother, looked down in surprise.

"Well, hello," she said, greeting the visitor with her customary warmth.

"Are you Suzanne Jackson?"

"Why, yes, I sure am. How may I help you?"

With an unexpected tug, the screen door opened and the woman —all five feet of her—brushed past Suzanne and marched straight into the house.

"Hey, wh-what are you doing?" a stunned Suzanne called after her.

The lady ignored her. "Is your father home?"

"No, he sure isn't."

"Good. Where's your computer?" It wasn't a question; it was a demand.

"*Tom!*" Suzanne cried out. Whenever someone thought of her, *confident* was the word that came to mind. She knew where she was going in life and wasn't easily rattled. But now, at this moment, her confidence had vanished. She couldn't figure out if she felt angry, scared, or both. But who could fear a five-foot-tall old lady?

Alarmed at his sister's tone, Tom raced downstairs as he threw on his bathrobe. "What's the matter, Suzie?"

"*This woman just walked right into our house!*" Suzanne hissed. "Like she owns it."

The older lady stood in the living room, her arms folded, refusing eye contact, appearing all but oblivious to the consternation around her.

Tom moved closer, forcing the stranger to focus on him. "What can we do for you?"

"Are you Tom Jackson?" She had an authoritative manner—like a person accustomed to issuing orders and always getting her own way.

"Yes, I am," he replied rather stiffly.

EXCERPT FROM BOOK 4

"Good," she said with a satisfied expression. "I need you both. Where's your computer?"

"It's right *there*," Suzanne said, her exasperation pouring into the open. Her face flushed as anger welled up inside her. She gestured to the corner desk in the living room, jabbing with an index finger. "Who *are* you, and what do you want with our computer?"

"I am Mrs. Leslie McPherson," the lady replied, drawing herself up as tall as she could with obvious pride. "And I don't *want* your stupid computer. I want to *show* you something."

"Okay," Tom said, but it wasn't. Quiet, thoughtful, and solid —"Like the Rock of Gibraltar, you can always count on him!" as one of his baseball coaches liked to say—Tom felt upended. He couldn't figure the woman out. She was, well, *odd*. Maybe worse. "There it is. Go for it."

"*You* go for it," she commanded. "Plug this thing in." An old-fashioned thumb drive appeared in her open hand.

That's when Tom's curiosity kicked into high gear. Technology of any kind, no matter how minor, intrigued him—he was a founding member of Prescott High's award-winning technology club. Tom plucked the drive from Mrs. McPherson's outstretched palm with two fingertips, trying his best not to touch her, all the while keeping a sharp eye on the woman. *No telling what she'll do next,* he thought, *but this is interesting.* He sat down at the desk and inserted the device in one of the laptop's USB ports.

Suzanne took a deep breath and calmed herself. Polite but guarded, she pulled over a loveseat behind her brother. "Please sit down," she said. Mrs. McPherson perched on the edge of the cushion, looking over Tom's shoulder. Suzanne joined her, keeping a safe distance between herself and their peculiar guest.

"There's only one file on it," Tom said, noting its format. "Video footage, I guess."

"Brilliant," the woman replied sharply. "Go to eleven twenty-eight."

The monitor lit up, displaying a grainy night scene: a wide-angle view of a parking lot and, across a two-lane roadway, an outdated-

EXCERPT FROM BOOK 4

looking single-story office building with a few vehicle spaces in front. A dull light shone out through the glass lobby doors. High above the building's entryway appeared a company name, McPherson Construction. The LED signage blazed in the darkness, casting a sickly green glow over the entire façade. The parking spots outlined on the asphalt, tight up against the structure, all sat empty.

Tom fast-forwarded a little, until the day/time stamp in the lower right corner of the screen read FRIDAY JUNE 8 11:28:00 PM. Seconds clicked by on the digital clock.

"Just last night?" Suzanne asked.

"Mmm-hmm," Mrs. McPherson replied.

"Is that your company?" Tom wondered aloud.

"What do you think?"

"There's no cause for rudeness," Suzanne said, ticked off again and letting it show. Mrs. McPherson, staring straight ahead, sniffed and ignored the admonition.

"What are we waiting for?" Tom asked.

On the screen, a car swooshed by in a blur along the two-lane street. Obviously, someone had installed a camera on the far side of the roadway.

"Patience," she replied.

Unseen by her, Tom rolled his eyes. Suzanne suppressed a wry smile.

A late-model Nissan sedan slowed and turned in. The driver skipped the parking places, pulling into deep shadows to the right of the building. If someone drove past, Tom noted—beat cops in a patrol car, for example—the vehicle would be all but invisible.

In the grainy footage, they watched the brake lights fade. A smallish man stepped into the night and hurried to the front door. It took a few seconds—he had a key—before the door swung open. He walked in, closing it after him, and disappearing down a dimly lit corridor.

It wasn't possible to see the man's face. Not once did he look back, and anyway the footage was far too grainy. The luminous signage threw off a steady glow, but visibility was marginal. The vehicle's rear license plate, sheltered from light, was unreadable.

"Who is he?" Suzanne asked.

"Philip Edward Marsden, and he's a con man and a thief."

Tom turned and locked eyes with her. "What did he do?"

"He robbed McPherson Construction—twice. The first time he stole a corporate entity we owned called Old Blue Dog Company. Then he hit us again—last night—which is what we're watching here. He helped himself to fifty-two hundred bucks and an antiquated computer."

"No way!" the twins chorused.

"Yup. The little maggot's building a nest somewhere," Mrs. McPherson said with certainty. She had a sarcastic manner of speaking, and a habit of talking with her hands, her arms flailing in the air.

"That's a lot of money," Suzanne said.

"You bet your life it is. He swiped it right out of my office safe, leaving it wide open. There's no doubt in my mind that he must have stolen the combination months ago. And Zeke lent him that computer—looks as if he wanted it back."

"So Marsden used to work for you?" Suzanne said. "And who's Zeke?"

Mrs. McPherson ignored the questions. She paused, seeming to gather her thoughts. "That's when it hit me: Philip Marsden has returned." She spoke tensely as her hands continued to bob and weave in the air. Suzanne slid further away on the loveseat to avoid getting whacked; the eccentric lady didn't even notice. "No rational soul would want that piece of computing junk—it's older than dirt."

"So he has a key to the building..." Suzanne said, wondering why.

"No kidding," Mrs. McPherson replied. "Turns out he made a copy before—now jump to eleven thirty-seven."

Tom scanned forward and hit *Play*. They watched as the same man stepped out the front door—a mid-size cardboard box tucked under one arm—and locked it behind him. He turned to look both

EXCERPT FROM BOOK 4

ways before slipping back to his car. Even then, the dark, grainy footage barred any possibility of identifying him. His face was nothing but a soft blur. Moments later, his vehicle backed out and zoomed away—still without affording clear visibility of its license plates.

Yet Mrs. McPherson plainly had no doubts as to the man's identity. "So last night, he came, he saw, he conquered," she quipped, deadpan. "Which, when you think about it, is bat-crazy weird."

"Why is that?" Tom asked, half afraid of what she'd say next.

"Because Philip Marsden died five weeks ago."

Hi, fellow mystery searchers!
I hope you enjoyed this sneak peek at
The House on Cemetery Hill.
Pick up a copy at your favorite retailer today!

And be sure to sign up for special deals
and to hear about new book releases before anyone else.
You can register here:

https://www.mysterysearchers.com/the-series/

BIOGRAPHY

Barry Forbes began his writing career in 1980, eventually scripting and producing hundreds of film and video corporate presentations, winning a handful of industry awards along the way. At the same time, he served as an editorial writer for Tribune Newspapers and wrote his first two books, both non-fiction.

In 1997, he founded and served as CEO for Sales Simplicity Software, a market leader which was sold two decades later.

What next? "I always loved mystery stories and one of my favorite places to visit was Prescott, Arizona. It's situated in rugged central Arizona with tremendous locales for mysteries." In 2017, Barry merged his interest in mystery and his skills in writing, adding in a large dollop of technology. The Mystery Searchers Family Book Series was born.

Barry's wife, Linda, passed in 2019 and the series is dedicated to her. "Linda proofed the initial drafts of each book and acted as my chief advisor." The couple had been married for 49 years and had two children. A number of their fifteen grandchildren provided feedback on each book.

Contact Barry: barry@mysterysearchers.com

ALSO BY BARRY FORBES

Book 1: The Mystery on Apache Canyon Drive

A small child wanders across a busy Arizona highway! In a hair-raising rescue, sixteen-year old twins Tom and Suzanne Jackson save the little girl from almost certain death. Soon, the brother and sister team up with best friends Kathy and Pete Brunelli on a perilous search for the child's past. The mystery deepens as one becomes two, forcing the deployment of secretive technology tools along Apache Canyon Drive. The danger level ramps up with the action, and the "mystery searchers" are born.

Book 2: The Ghost in the County Courthouse

A mysterious "ghost" bypasses the security system of Yavapai Courthouse Museum and makes off with four of the museum's most precious Native American relics. The mystery searchers, at the invitation of curator Dr. William Wasson, jump into the case and deploy a range of technology tools to discover the ghost's secrets. If the ghost strikes again, the museum's very future is in doubt. A dangerous game of cat and mouse ensues.

Book 3: The Secrets of the Mysterious Mansion

Heidi Hoover, a good friend and newspaper reporter for *The Daily Pilot*, introduces the mystery searchers to a mysterious mansion in the forest—at midnight! The mansion is under siege from unknown "hunters." *Who are they? What are they searching for?* Good, old-fashioned detective work and a couple of technology tools ultimately reveal the truth. A desperate race ensues, but time is running out.

Book 4: The House on Cemetery Hill

There's a dead man walking and it's up to the mystery searchers to figure out "why." That's the challenge from Mrs. Leslie McPherson, a successful but eccentric Prescott businesswoman. The mystery searchers team up with their favorite detective and utilize technology to spy on high-tech criminals at Cemetery Hill. It's a perilous game with heart-stopping moments.

Book 5: The Treasure of Skull Valley

Suzanne discovers a map hidden in the pages of a classic old book at the thrift store. It's titled "My Treasure Map" and leads past Skull Valley, twenty miles west of Prescott and into the high desert country—to an unexpected, shocking and elusive treasure. "Please help," the note begs. The mystery searchers utilize the power and reach of the Internet to trace the movement of people and events. . . half a century earlier.

Book 6: The Vanishing in Deception Gap

A text message to Kathy sets off a race into the unknown. "There are pirates operating out here and they're dangerous. I can't prove it, but I need your help." Who sent the message? Out where? Pirates! How weird is that? The mystery searchers dive in, but it might be too late. *The man has vanished into thin air.*

Book 7: The Heist Forgotten by Time

Coming – Fall/Winter, 2020

Don't forget to check out
www.MysterySearchers.com

Register to receive *free* parent/reader study guides for each book in the series—valuable teaching and learning tools for middle-grade students and their parents.

You'll also find a wealth of information on the website: stills and video scenes of Prescott, reviews, press releases, awards, and more. Plus, I'll update you on new book releases and other news.

Made in the USA
Monee, IL
05 October 2022

93b173f3-1e25-46c2-8d98-e960a5d27de2R01